Uncanny Collateral

UNCANNY COLLATERAL

BRIAN MCCLELLAN

All material contained within copyright © Brian McClellan, 2019.

All rights reserved.

This is a work of fiction. All names, characters, places and scenarios are either products of the author's imagination or used fictitiously. All resemblance to actual persons, living or dead, is purely coincidental.

Typesetting and ebook conversion by handebooks.co.uk.

Chapter 1

It was a cool spring evening as I sat in my truck in the middle of nowhere, Pennsylvania, watching the parking lot of a run-down bikers' bar gradually fill up with leather-chap-wearing skinheads. I lay with my head against the doorframe of the open driver's-side window and my feet on the dashboard. A local '80s station crackled through my radio, and an almost-empty bag of honey-roasted cashews rested in the crook of my arm. I kept my baseball cap pulled low. To the casual observer, I was just a drunk sleeping off an early bender.

I scratched at the tattoo of Mjolnir on the back of my right hand, trying to remember what the local cops had said about this place. As far as I could tell, it didn't even have a proper name, just a generic white sign that said BAR in large red letters. It was owned by a gang who called themselves the Dirty Imps. They ran a few rackets around town: meth, weed, and a little bit of protection. They weren't terribly ambitious, though, and spent more of their time fishing at the local reservoir than getting up to petty crime.

There's an imp taking a piss in the woods back there, a voice said in my head. The voice belonged to a woman and held a hint of a dozen different accents that all seemed to attach themselves to different words; it was a lyrical sound that came off as both young and incredibly old.

The old guy with the beard and leather vest? I answered. *I thought he went inside.*

Not a biker. An actual imp.

Slowly, I reached up and tilted my rearview mirror. I caught sight of a thin, bald figure standing a few dozen yards behind the truck, head tilted back in that way tired men often did when they relieved themselves. After a few moments, the figure looked down, gave one leg a good shake, and headed back inside, passing my open window close enough that I could have reached out and touched him.

The imp was about five feet tall—few grew taller than that—and wore jeans and a flannel shirt with the sleeves rolled up. Like most imps, he had large ears, a small nose, and the emaciated look and gross vibe of a meth addict. The average human, whether or not they can recognize an imp on sight, naturally avoids them. I snorted. *I've never seen an imp in flannel before. What's he doing out here anyway? I thought they normally keep to the cities.*

He washes dishes for the kitchen of the bar.

Will he be an issue?

Nope.

Then why did you bring him to my attention?

Because I know how much you hate imps.

I sighed and put the imp out of my mind. *He's not my problem.*

All right, all right, the voice answered defensively. *Just trying to be helpful.*

You're the most helpful person I know. It wasn't a lie, either. Maggie could be easily distracted—especially on stakeouts—but she'd saved my life a dozen times. She and I were partners of a sort—the accidental, unwilling-but-making-the-best-of-it sort. A few years back, when I was young and dumb, I put on a ring I found in a debtor's cash box. The ring didn't come off—still won't. Just as surely as I'm trapped wearing the ring, Maggie is trapped *inside* the ring. Jinn are desert spirits who long for the freedom of big, empty stretches of wilderness. They don't want to be stuck on the finger of a working schmuck based out of Cleveland, Ohio.

Maggie's reply was cut off by the sound of big engines coming up the road. A few moments later, a trio of men parked their Harleys on the far side of the lot. I ignored two of them, focusing on the tallest of the three. William Hadley—or Dirty Billy, according to police blotters—looked about six foot three and forty years old, with an ample beer belly. Billy wore leather chaps over jeans, a black leather vest, no helmet, and he sported a short goatee and a shaved head.

I didn't bother to check the picture on my phone. *He, I* told Maggie, *is my problem.* I slowly eased up in my seat and waited until the big biker and his companions had gone inside before I stepped out of the car. *Keep your eyes peeled. If more of Billy's friends show up, let me know ASAP.* I touched Maggie's ring out of habit, then made sure my Glock was secure in my shoulder holster. I didn't *think* I'd need it, but better safe than sorry.

The inside of the bar was dimly lit by neon beer signs. A handful of fans spun on the low ceiling, unsuccessfully attempting to dispel the stank of some thirty bodies drinking heavily in a small space. I paused for a moment just inside the door to get my bearings and immediately spotted Billy's two companions jawing with the bartender. Billy himself was gone. There weren't any other exits aside from a single door leading off the bar and into the back room.

He went into the back, Maggie told me.

So I gathered.

No need for sarcasm; I was just making sure.

I eyed that door as I slid up to the bar and grinned at the bartender, setting my wallet down in front of me.

"What can I get ya?" the bartender asked.

"Something local. I'm looking for Billy Hadley."

The bartender snorted. "What are you, an undercover cop or something? Never seen a cop dressed like that."

"Not in the slightest." I opened my wallet and pulled out a business card. It was white with black lettering that said *Valkyrie Collections: We Deal with Mortals So You Don't Have To.* My name and cell phone number were on the back. "Do me a favor and give him this. Tell him his debt is past due, and it would be a good idea if he talked to me tonight."

The bartender didn't look at the card. "Billy doesn't owe

anyone."

"That you know of."

"He's not here."

I stretched. Not a lot—just enough physical theater so that the bartender got the idea that I was much larger than him. I've got troll somewhere back in my foggy, northern European ancestry. It's diluted enough that I get a few good perks without being as dumb as a brick or turning to stone in sunlight. I'm six foot four with broad shoulders, short blond hair, a strawberry beard, and a bunch of tattoos. I look like I hit the gym every day, though I definitely do not. I like to think I have a Tom Hardy thing going on. Maggie says I look more like a techno Viking. In short, my clients like the fact that I look like a guy you shouldn't mess with.

"I watched him walk in three minutes ago," I yawned. "Go give him my card."

The bartender tried to stare me down for a few long seconds. I responded with the same look I give to salesmen who try to get me to buy their shit before I've had my fifth cup of coffee in the morning. He finally broke off his stare, took my card, and headed into the back room.

I leaned across the bar and snagged an unopened bottle of some import I'd never heard of.

God, I haven't had a beer in forever, Maggie said.

I thought you could conjure just about anything you want inside that little world of yours. Beer was a new complaint. She usually moaned about not being able to get laid or get a massage. I was pretty good at sympathizing, considering that I was a slave to my boss—she *literally* owned me. Maggie and I were both trapped in places we didn't want to be.

I can, but it's not the same.

There isn't any way I can just, like, hand you one, is there?

There was a long silence. *No one has ever offered before. I spend all my time trying to get out. It never occurred to me to try to bring* things *into* this place.

How did you get your library in there?

It came with me when I was cursed. My whole villa did. I'll give it some thought.

Seven centuries, and life can still surprise you, I told her. I genuinely hoped she could figure it out. Life without beer? Hardly sounded worth living.

I'd barely managed a few swallows of my pilfered drink before the bartender returned. He flicked my card in my face, then snatched the beer out of my hand. "Excuse me?" I said. The gums around my bottom canines began to ache, and it took a brief force of will to keep my tusks from emerging. "I planned on paying for that."

"You're not paying for anything. Billy says that if you aren't out of here in thirty seconds, you're going to wake up tomorrow without any teeth."

"Ah." I kept the smile plastered to my face and stepped back from the bar. "I see how it is. You don't think he'll reconsider?"

"Twenty seconds."

"Right." I took five dollars out of my wallet and put it in the tip cup. "One quick question?"

"Real quick."

"Do you have a restroom?"

The flick of the bartender's eyes toward that one door was all I needed. "Not that you can use," the bartender growled. "You be out that door in five seconds."

"Okay, okay!" I held up my hands. "I'm going!"

I stepped outside, breathing a deep lungful of the humid spring night, and held the door open for an older woman heading inside. I massaged the gums around my lower canines. Once—just once—I wished these assholes could do things the easy way. But then again, my job wasn't to collect the easy debts.

I could have told you where the restroom was, Maggie said.

Asking basic questions of idiots is the only social life I have. Leave me that, please.

A sharp pain like a bee sting stabbed my finger beneath Maggie's ring. *The* only *social life you have?*

You know exactly what I meant, I shot back.

Hmph. See if I warn you the next time someone is about to shoot you in the back.

I chuckled at Maggie's faux anger and walked around the side of the building, where I took out my wallet, flipping it open flat in my hand. My job sends me into some pretty shady places; I run into stolen goods and ancient stockpiles of loot both magical and mundane fairly often. Most of those are turned over to the proper authorities, but some of them "accidentally" make their way home with me. Maggie's ring was one such item. My endless wallet is another. It's one of the few decent perks of my job.

I fished through the interior of a space much larger than any earthly billfold and pulled out a mirror the size of a checkbook. The mirror, unlike the wallet, was standard gear. It allowed me to move between it and another nearby mirror. I glanced over my shoulder and continued around to the back of the building, where I spotted a tiny restroom window. Just beneath it, I slapped the mirror against the wall. Instead of shattering on contact, the glass stuck to the cinder block as if glued in place. With one more look around, I pressed my fingers to the glass.

I blinked. The world seemed to crinkle around me, and suddenly I was standing in a tiny restroom. It reeked of piss, its once-white walls now off-yellow. A single bare light bulb flickered above my head.

"Charming," I muttered and opened the door.

The restroom let out into a cluttered office with two grimy couches, a scratched pool table, and a desk shoved into one corner. Papers, discarded food, and old clothes seemed to cover every surface. My target sat on one of the couches, his beer belly peeking out from under his stained shirt and a *definitely* too-young-for-him woman sitting on his lap.

"Who the hell are you?" Billy demanded.

"Out," I told the woman, snatching her by the arm and shoving her out the office door. I locked it behind her and turned to face Billy, who was struggling to get out of the sagging couch.

"Just what the hell—"

"My name is Alek Fitz," I said. "I'm a reaper for Valkyrie Collections, and I've come to collect your debt."

The word *debt* was barely out of my mouth when Billy's eyes grew wide. He lunged for the desk, jerking open one of the drawers. I was there a second later, glimpsing the gun concealed within. I slammed the drawer closed on Billy's hand, then a fist into his gut. No need to use magic on this one.

Billy doubled over, caught himself on one of the couches, and swung at me. I sidestepped the punch and grabbed Billy by the elbow. I like to practice finesse over force when I'm able. Two decades of jujitsu allowed me to do just that. I leaned away, crossed a leg behind Billy's, and put the big biker on his back.

You've got company, Maggie warned, *and he's armed.*

Someone pounded on the door, and I recognized the bartender's voice. "Billy? Is everything okay in there?"

With what? I asked.

Twelve-gauge shotgun.

Thanks to my troll heritage, buckshot wasn't going to pierce my skin even at close range. But it sure would hurt like hell. I quickly knelt beside Billy, turning Maggie's ring around so the ruby faced inward, and then cupped the side of Billy's head. I could sense a trickle of Maggie's sorcery warm my finger. "You feel that burning sensation on the side of your scalp?" Billy tried to get up. I put one knee on his sternum. "If you try to move one more time, I'm going to set your head on fire. Understand?"

Billy swallowed hard and lay still.

With one hand, I pulled out my wallet and managed to produce another mirror. This one was smaller—about the size of a credit card—and had a red thumbprint in one corner. I turned it over to read the tiny, immaculate handwriting on the back.

"William Hadley," I intoned, "I am here to collect on a debt four years, three months, and two days past due. I do so with the full authority of the contract you made with my client, LuciCorp, and the authority of the Rules that bind mankind and the Other." I ran my eyes over the script, making sure I hadn't left out any important details, and paused when I got to the terms of the contract. I read it again. Then I leaned over, looking Billy in the eye and ignoring the pounding on the office door. "You sold your soul for a 'bitchin' motorcycle'? You're an even bigger asshole than I thought."

I adjusted my left hand, grabbed Billy by the face, forced open his right eye with two fingers, then thrust the mirror in front of his eye. The effect was immediate; Billy went rigid for a handful of seconds, then began to thrash and convulse like he'd been hit with a stun gun. I held him down until the count of five, then got up and stashed the mirror in my wallet. He gave out a low, pain-filled moan.

"That's gonna hurt for a few weeks," I advised. "I recommend icing your temples and avoiding alcohol." He didn't *actually* need to avoid alcohol, but I enjoy giving advice to people who are just gonna ignore it anyway. I didn't personally know what it was like to live without a soul, but I'd heard it was terrible. I nudged him with my toe. "You hear me?"

You're out of time, Maggie said, an instant before the door burst open. I caught a glance of the grizzled bartender, Billy's frightened girlfriend, and the barrel of a shotgun.

"Shit," I spat, leaping for the bathroom door.

I heard the blast of the gun, but then my fingers touched

the bathroom mirror and I was back outside the rear of the bar. Ears ringing, I grabbed my stepping mirror off the wall and sprinted for my truck. Within seconds I was flying down the highway, one eye on the rearview mirror and another on the road as I fumbled for my phone.

My call rang twice before a woman picked up. "Ada, it's Alek."

"You get it?" The voice on the other end sounded exactly what one might expect a two-pack-a-day smoker to sound like, which I always find funny because Ada doesn't smoke.

"Let OtherOps know I reaped a soul off of William Hadley in Mercer County," I told her.

"Any trouble?"

"Shotgun. He missed."

"Good. I'm not paying for another company polo."

Have I told you your boss is a bitch? Maggie interjected.

I ignored her and bit my tongue so that I wouldn't tell Ada to go to hell. Company polo? Really? "I'll have you know I was wearing a hoodie tonight."

If Ada heard the joke in my tone, she ignored it. "Those are even more expensive."

I sighed. "Right. Thanks for the concern. It'll take me a couple hours to get home. I'll be in late tomorrow."

"You'll do no such thing. You have an appointment at six AM sharp."

"You're shitting me."

Huuuuuuge bitch, Maggie whispered.

"Be there," Ada ordered.

"Ada! It's Friday night. I've been working eighteen-hour days. Give me a goddamned break."

The word *break* had barely left my mouth when I felt an intense pain in my chest. My left arm went numb, and I gasped for breath, barely managing to get out the words "Yes, ma'am. I'll be there at six."

I have a lot of tattoos. Some of them are for show. Others,

like the tattoo of Mjolnir on my right hand and Grendel's claw on my left, are reaper specials that allow me to dish out some serious damage. There's one, though, that is completely unique. On the left side of my chest, just above my heart, is a barcode about an inch long. It was put there when I was an infant, after my parents sold me. Since Ada owns me now, she has control of that little tattoo, and she can do some mean things with its sorcery.

The pain went away instantly, lingering as a memory—a reminder—in my chest. "Good," Ada said. "And don't fuck this up. It's important."

"Who am I meeting with?"

"Death."

"Oh." I hung up the phone and stared at the road. I could feel Maggie stalking around in the back of my head. Ada's abuse always put her in a foul mood. I think it made her feel as helpless as I did.

When she'd finally calmed down, Maggie asked, *Was Ada serious about meeting Death?*

In all the time you've been riding along with me, has Ada ever made a joke? I responded, driving with one hand clutching my chest. I wasn't thrilled about the idea myself. I'd met all manner of magical beings in my line of work, including a handful of minor gods. But Death, the Great Constant? This was new. Even Lucy was wary of Death, and *she'd* been giving Yahweh the finger for six thousand years.

What are you going to do? Maggie asked.

I'm going to be at my meeting on time, I told her, *and I'm not going to shake his hand.*

Chapter 2

I woke up after a few hours of restless sleep. I live in a rotting little one-bedroom cottage—a former servant's quarters—in the far corner of one of the big estates in Gates Mills. It belongs to wealthy friend of Ada's, and it should probably be condemned. Aside from the necessary furniture, I've got a tube TV with a couple of old gaming stations, a work laptop, and nothing on the walls except for a little picture shrine to Avalanche, the white golden retriever I had when I was a teenager. The rooms are clean, the fridge always empty. I don't get to spend a lot of time there, but it's home.

I stared, bleary-eyed, around my bedroom, trying to remember my own name, until Ada's instructions rolled through my foggy memory and I dragged myself out of bed. After a quick shower and a comb of the beard, I headed to work.

I arrived in the Valkyrie parking lot at quarter till six. The lot was empty except for the cruiser of a rent-a-cop sitting idling by the entrance. Ted, the rent-a-cop, gave me a wave and returned to whatever book he was reading while I pulled into my spot and stared in irritation at the still-dark building.

Valkyrie works out of a two-story brick office off Route 20 in Wickliffe, Ohio. It has the advantages of dirt-cheap rent and being close to two major highways—the former of which was probably foremost in Ada's mind when she chose the location. Since a lot of debtors take our work personally, the building is protected by a state-of-the-art security system, half a dozen wards against various evils and, of course, Ted, who I enjoy referring to as a rent-a-cop, but who was a Navy SEAL for twelve years and in the Secret Service for five. He's heavily armed enough to take on a pack of werewolves single-handed, and I'd be surprised if he's entirely human.

You awake? I asked Maggie. She claims she needs sleep almost as much as I do, but I think she just does it to pass the time.

Just having my coffee, she answered. *Or what passes for coffee in this place.*

I'm so tired I almost crashed three times just getting here.

I missed that, she replied. *You want me to give you a little pick-me-up?*

I eyed the building. My client would arrive soon. *I have to be in top shape for this meeting. So yeah, you'd better give me a jolt.*

A tiny bit of warmth trickled out through Maggie's ring. It was pleasant at first, then quickly followed by a sensation that I can only describe as having a needle rammed underneath a fingernail. It spread through my body like a wave, hitting me hard for less than a second before disappearing, leaving me with the memory of the pain—and more awake than I'd been in weeks.

Lord, I always forget how much that hurts.

Don't be a baby, she responded.

I headed inside, using a good old-fashioned key to open up the building. I walked past the empty reception desk and across the dark collection room. Rows of cubicles filled the entire first floor. In a few hours they would be buzzing with conversation as the day team arrived to do cold calls and skip tracing. They were our first line of offense against the wayward debtor, and they managed to bring in about eighty-two percent of what was owed to our clients just by getting in contact and reminding people they had debts to pay.

The other eighteen percent? That's where I come in.

I punched in a code on the door at the other end of the room and headed up a narrow staircase to the second floor, where I flipped on all the lights and put on a pot of coffee. The second floor had a bank of eight offices down one side—one for each of our full-time reapers—opposite a large corner office, a break room, and our secretary's cubby.

I was the only one in at this hour on a weekend, of course. None of the other reapers were literally company property.

Hey, so... it's my anniversary next week, Maggie said.

I froze in the middle of opening a Ho Ho for breakfast. *Shit, Mags,* I said. *I didn't realize it was coming up so soon.*

Think you can get the day off?

Despite the fact that Maggie practically lived in my head, she'd always been standoffish about her past. I'd quickly learned not to ask too many questions, which meant that I knew a lot less about her than she did about me. Not an ideal situation, but there wasn't much I could do about it. There's a certain class of Other that you don't get pushy with unless you have to, and jinn definitely qualify.

This meant that I didn't know the exact circumstances of her imprisonment in the ring. From what I'd gathered, she got into a fight with a magician masquerading as a priest and ended up in her current predicament. Somehow she'd managed to get a single day of freedom each year on the anniversary of her imprisonment. I wasn't entirely certain whether that was through her own sorcery or some sort of twisted mind game on the part of the magician, but Maggie liked to use that day to do things she couldn't experience within the ring.

Last year, we spent thirteen hours playing Frisbee golf, ate a steak dinner, and then I wing-manned for her at the bars so she could get laid.

I'll try, I told her. *You know how Ada is about that kind of thing. What do you want to do?*

There was a pause. *I'm not sure.*

Yes, you are. You have all year to think about it. What do you want to do?

Bowling, maybe?

I could sense she wasn't telling me what she really wanted—probably because it was too expensive. Unlike the rest of the reapers, Ada paid *me* just enough to get by, so I usually had to raid my change jar each year so Maggie could do something fun. *We went bowling two years ago. Come on, just tell me.*

I want to go to the beach, came the answer.

This is Cleveland. The beaches here suck.

I know. I want to go to a real beach.

That's why she didn't want to tell me. Money was tight, but time was even tighter. Getting a single day off from Ada was like pulling teeth. Getting two or three days—enough to drive somewhere with proper sand and waves—was like asking for the moon.

I caught the scent of cigarette smoke and frowned, looking around the office for the source. None of the windows were open, and none of my coworkers were there. I walked down the hall, following my nose until I noticed smoke curling out from beneath Ada's office door. Since Ada was a nonsmoker, I knew it couldn't be hers. *He's here,* I said to Maggie. *I'll see what I can do about the beach, but no promises. Try to think of a backup plan.*

I opened the door to Ada's office and coughed as I was enveloped in a cloud of cigarette smoke so thick it made my eyes water. I could see nothing in the darkness except for the glow of a single ember in the center of Ada's chair. I flipped on the lights.

An old man sat behind Ada's desk. For a moment, I thought that Keith Richards had rolled his greasy ass out of Beverly Hills to come meet with me. The figure was as thin as a rail, with a sun-wrinkled face; long, stringy white hair; and yellowed nails at the ends of bony fingers. He looked like someone who'd managed to try and survive every drug known to man over a long and storied life.

His feet were on the desk, the chair tilted back. He wore ripped jeans, unlaced construction boots, and an AC/DC T-shirt with Angus Young rocking out on the front.

"This is a no-smoking building," I told him.

He cocked an eyebrow. "You know who I am?"

"If you have to ask…" I said, coming to sit opposite him.

"Then either you don't actually care, or I'm not that important," he finished, grinning at me through cracked lips. He crushed the cigarette out on Ada's desk and removed his feet, leaning forward in her chair to examine me with black irises. No, not black—flecked, like a dark galaxy of stars. "Ada told me you were unflappable."

To be honest, I was more than a little impressed—not at his outfit, but his sheer presence. It filled the room, expanding to every corner like the smoke of his cigarettes. Both my human *and* troll sides could sense it, and that meant something. "Not unflappable," I said, "but my boss can make my life miserable when she finds out someone smoked in her office. You… well, all you can do is kill me."

He rolled his eyes. "If I had a nickel for every time someone's said that… I don't actually kill people. I just usher them from one world to the next." His voice was a guttural purr, like Bob Dylan's on a good day.

"I know, but I didn't get up at five in the morning to argue semantics with Death."

Would you get a load of this guy? I asked Maggie.

Oh, I have, she answered in a whisper. *And I can't believe you're talking back to him. Show some fucking respect, Alek.*

Is the big, bad jinn scared of her own mortality? I teased.

I'm serious.

That sobered me up. For a reasonably powerful Other, Maggie tends to be pretty cautious. I think it's a consequence of being stuck in a tiny portable house on a mortal's finger. While she knows that I can handle myself, she's never been shy about reining me in when I'm being stupid. *Is he the real deal?* I asked. *Like, actually Death and not some underling or avatar?*

Yeah, it's him. He gives me the heebie-jeebies.

I smiled at my new client. "I'm sorry for the snark," I said, "but it's kind of an early hour. Let's start this off on the right foot. My name is Alek Fitz. I'm the lead reaper at Valkyrie.

I'm guessing that you're Death?

He seemed more amused than offended. "You can call me Ferryman," he responded. "It's less..."

"Ominous?" I suggested.

"Just so."

I leaned back in my chair, hands in my hoodie pocket, considering something that had been on my mind ever since Ada told me who I'd be meeting with. "Forgive me, sir, but I didn't know you *were* a client."

"I wasn't until last night."

"Let me rephrase that: I didn't know you had the capacity to be our client. As far as I'm aware, you don't trade with humans."

"Correct."

"Then why are you here?"

Ferryman watched me for a few moments with those disconcerting eyes, then produced a lighter from his pocket and tapped it on the table. I wouldn't have imagined Death as a nervous smoker. He said, "Do you know the difference between a soul, a spirit, and a shade?"

From the way he said the words, I assumed they were technical terms rather than nebulous ideas. "I know what a soul is. The others sound above my pay grade."

"They are. Your spirit is the thing that exists before and after your time in this mortal realm. When you're born, it's split into two pieces—the soul and the shade. The soul comes with you into mortality. The shade remains here." He gestured to the darkness around him. "Part of my job as Ferryman is to reunite soul and shade and send the entire spirit off to wherever it's meant to go."

All of this was news to me. I *had* wondered what goes on before and after death—I'm still human, after all. But the Other doesn't always make sense in human terms, so thinking about it too much is often a good route to a bad headache. "You're an administrator?"

"I'd probably romanticize it a little more than that, but essentially, yes."

I pursed my lips at the explanation, annoyed that he wouldn't give me a straight answer. "Then," I asked again, more emphatically, *"why are you here?"* In the back of my head, Maggie had gone quiet. From her ring, I could feel her presence like a person with their ear pressed against the door.

"Because souls are missing."

I watched him carefully, waiting for the *and* attached to the end of that sentence. Missing souls were my job, but I got the very clear sense from his cageyness that this wasn't the run-of-the-mill "old debtor took off running" kind of job. Something was up. If he didn't have my attention before, he definitely had it now.

"From where?"

"From the vaults of a number of your clients."

I scoffed. "Is that possible?" As far as I had ever been aware, once Beelzebub or whoever got their claws onto your soul—sometimes with my help—that soul was theirs until further notice. It had never even occurred to me that they *could* be stolen.

"It is possible," Ferryman answered, "and it has happened."

"Is there an illicit trade in souls?"

"There isn't. The souls literally don't have value in this life. Once they've been reunited with the shade and move on as part of the whole spirit, *then* they have value. The reason *you* have a job," he said, pointing one long finger at me, "is because the physical possession of a soul upon the death of the mortal vessel is extremely important in determining where the spirit winds up." Ferryman sighed, clearly getting tired of my line of questioning. "*I'm* here because most of your clients have been robbed. So many are affected, they've asked me to be their proxy. Is that satisfactory?"

"Yes," I answered. It wasn't; I still had a bunch of questions. But if Ferryman wanted to get on with business, I had little choice but to go along with it. I'm just a working peon, after all. "How many souls?"

"Two hundred seventeen," he answered sharply.

"Jesus… man, I go after maybe one a week at most!"

Ferryman snorted a laugh. "These aren't debtors you're after; they're souls. You *should* find them contained in the same kind of soul mirrors that you use for collecting."

"All right," I said, gathering my thoughts. This was a little unorthodox. Usually I was chasing a debtor—a person I could track. Stolen goods was out of my comfort zone, which led me to another question: "Why are you coming to a reaper agency? This sounds like it should be handed over to OtherOps." OtherOps is to the cops what reapers are to monetary debt collectors. A reaper maintains the *contractual* balance between the Other and humanity. OtherOps deals with anything that can't be solved by the wording on a piece of paper. Theft certainly fell under that.

Ferryman seemed to consider his response. "The Lords of Hell have requested that OtherOps not be involved. Not yet, anyway. Missing souls are bad for business. They want discretion, which is something OtherOps doesn't do well."

Most normal people think of the Other as forces of nature—creatures or entities to be tolerated, worshiped, or sometimes controlled, but generally out of mind unless humans were directly confronted with something they couldn't explain. People expect OtherOps to protect them from the more dangerous aspects of the Other and to clean up quickly when there's an incident. Unfortunately, OtherOps is a mostly human organization, which makes it rife with human failings. They let stuff slip through the cracks and leak things to the press all the time, so Ferryman certainly had a point.

I tapped one of my lower canines with a fingernail, trying to think of what else I'd need to know before I got started. "Do we know *how* the souls went missing?"

"A number of different storage facilities were burgled at the end of last summer. No two of the facilities are owned by the same Lord of Hell, so they didn't pick up on the pattern or even the thefts until their spring audit."

"How did they not notice the thefts?" I asked suspiciously.

Ferryman shrugged. "They handle a lot of souls. Would you notice five or six candies missing from a family-sized pack of M&M's?"

Is he telling the truth? I asked Maggie.

She responded with a snort. *Shit, I don't know. My lie detector works on humans and most of the lesser Others, not the Great Constant himself.*

Something about this sounds fishy, I said. *I've met Lucy and most of her siblings. They don't let souls fall through the cracks.*

I don't disagree, Maggie responded.

I gave Ferryman a considering look and decided not to call him out. He was paying the bills. If he wasn't concerned by the circumstance, then I wasn't either. "Okay, just a couple more questions and I'll get started. Why me?"

"Because you're the best in the business," Ferryman responded, frowning at me as if it should be obvious.

"I'm flattered," I answered sarcastically. (I was, actually, a little flattered.) "Has Hell conducted its own investigations yet?"

"As far as it can without breaking the Rules," Ferryman said. "They've come up with nothing. The best we can give you is that the souls were all stolen from facilities in the Great Lakes region, so you'll be working locally."

I'd actually been looking forward to the idea of getting out of town, but I nodded along. "That's good. To be clear, the original owners of these souls know nothing about this?"

"They're not to be bothered," Ferryman confirmed.

"And none of these stolen souls have popped up anywhere?"

"Not a single one." Ferryman's twitchy fingers finally got the better of him, and he lit up another cigarette. He took a drag, then added, "I need you to find these souls quickly and quietly. The Rules prevent the Lords of Hell from dirtying their hands. You, on the other hand, are free to do as needed."

Now, *that* was interesting. I'd never actually had carte blanche before. "Is that right? If I actually have to kill people over this, will you keep OtherOps off my back? Because the last thing I need is to do a job for you and then get swarmed by the cops."

"I'll make sure they don't interfere."

He didn't answer your question, Maggie pointed out. I repeated the thought aloud.

Ferryman cracked the slightest smile. "All right. I'll make sure that whatever you have to do in my employ has no consequences."

"Then I think we can work together."

"I'm relieved," Ferryman said with a wan smile. "I already paid Ada a deposit."

"I'll get started immediately. If I have to contact you with questions…?"

Ferryman rotated his wrist, producing a card like some cheap street magician. It was black with red lettering that said, in a heavy-metal-style font, the word DEATH. Awfully subtle, that. There was a phone number beneath it. The card was thick and heavy, and on the back was a mirror.

"Stepping mirror?" I asked.

"The phone number goes to an answering service. The mirror goes directly to my realm in case you need to speak with me personally. If that's all, I should be going."

"That's all," I confirmed.

The lights flickered, and Ferryman was gone in the space of a blink, leaving behind the strong smell of cigarettes and the fading, uneasy feeling of his presence. I eyed the empty chair for a few moments, repeating the conversation in my head as I tried to think of somewhere to start this investigation.

I may not be able to read him like I can a human, Maggie said to me, *but I can tell he's* pissed *and hiding it well.*

You think that means something? I asked.

I don't think Death normally cares much for emotion. The fact this has made him genuinely angry means it's serious.

"Well, shit," I said aloud. I took out my phone and punched Ada's number. She picked up after a single ring, and I could imagine her sitting in her Parisian hotel room, long nails drumming on the desk while she waited for my call.

"Well?" she asked.

"How's the business trip going?"

"Splendidly. How is Death?"

"I just finished my meeting."

"And?"

"And I have the details. I'll get started now. I'm gonna go out on a limb and guess he's paying you a shitload for this side job."

"Your point?"

"My point is that I should probably work this job twenty-four seven."

"Yes," she responded. "I'll have Nadine put all your other jobs on hold for the time being."

"My other point is that I want the weekend of the eighteenth off of work."

Silence. I could hear her irritation in the cadence of her breathing. I wasn't really in a position to negotiate, but I was doing it anyway. Whether that would annoy her or amuse her was a coin toss. "Finish this job quickly," she said, "and we'll talk." She hung up.

I eyed my phone for a moment. *You hear that?* I asked Maggie.

Yeah. She will genuinely consider your request if you polish this thing off. I could hear it in her voice. Maggie let out a little whoop. *Fuck, yeah! Let's find this thieving asshole, and then, beaches, here we come.*

I grinned and hid my reservations from Maggie. Ada wasn't shy about sending me on the most dangerous jobs—it's why she bought a troll-blooded child two decades ago, after all. The fact that Death had involved himself personally meant that this could get hairy—really hairy—and I couldn't help but wonder how many details he was hiding from me.

It was time to get to work and find out.

Chapter 3

My first move was to find myself a better lead. "Someone in the Great Lakes area is stealing souls" wasn't going to be very useful. I considered putting a few of our company skip tracers on the job, but I didn't even have a name to start them off on. And since Ferryman had stressed discretion, that meant I was on my own. Anyone I told about this thing had to be trustworthy.

I stopped by an ATM before hitting the hour-long drive to southern Akron, where I found a busy, pothole-pitted street and parked in front of a corner pawnshop with a sign above it declaring ZEKE'S PAWN AND CHARITY. A green neon lotto sign in the window blinked on and off.

A bell rang as I stepped into the shop's cool darkness. The establishment was devoid of customers and overwhelmed by piles of junk on every available surface. Some items had handwritten price tags, while others were stacked on shelves labeled BEST OFFER. The place smelled of dust and salami, and I fought back a sneeze as I looked over a glass case full of jewelry and wondered how much of it was stolen.

I don't know why you always come here first, Maggie said. *Zeke is a weirdo.*

I rolled my eyes. *I come here because Zeke finds out everything going on around town faster than just about anyone else I know.*

So? Shouldn't you boycott his services? I thought that's what decent people do.

Just because you don't like him?

Yes, she answered without a trace of irony.

Zeke gets me results. Results get you to the beach next week.

Point taken.

I suppressed a smile, then went to the glass case of knickknacks at the very end of the room and banged on the top. "Zeke, you have a customer! Stop watching soaps and get out here!"

"Hold on, hold on," a voice answered from the back. There was a crash followed by a litany of swear words, and then a short, balding man with tufts of black hair sticking out from the sides of his head emerged from the back room. He wore a dirty X-men T-shirt and carried a coffee mug that reeked of bourbon from six paces away. I frowned and squinted.

That's new, Maggie said.

"Zeke?" I asked.

"Heya, Alek! How are you doing this fine day?" he answered cheerfully, slamming the coffee cup on the counter top so hard that I was surprised the glass didn't shatter. "I was just about to give you a call."

I opened my mouth, closed it, and gave him a long, hard look. "Zeke, why do you look like Danny DeVito?"

He stared at me like I was an idiot for a moment before smacking his head. "You haven't seen me since I changed last, have you?"

"The last time I saw you, you were taller than me. And Indian."

Zeke is a retired angel. A cherubim, to be exact. He claims he stood guard outside the Garden of Eden and all that jazz, but even with Maggie in my ring, I don't trust his stories. I knew that he changed looks every few decades so that the locals didn't get suspicious, but I'd never actually seen him do it.

"Right," he responded, leaning across the table and whispering in a conspiratorial tone. "Look, if anyone comes in here looking for Zeke, just call me Fred. I had to change a little early this time because I got in deep with some loan sharks in Canton." He straightened and grinned. "So 'Fred' bought out Zeke's Pawn and Charity."

"And Zeke fled the country?" I guessed.

"Exactly."

I told you he's fucking weirdo, Maggie whispered.

"Why Danny DeVito?" I asked.

Zeke cocked an eyebrow. "Who's Danny DeVito?"

Oh, lord, Maggie said. *He's not kidding around. He has no idea who Danny DeVito is.*

I sighed. "You picked this look by accident?"

"I'm not sure what you mean."

"Ever heard of *It's Always Sunny in Philadelphia*?"

"Sounds familiar."

"How about *Taxi*?"

Zeke's eyes lit up. "I think I've got that on VHS somewhere around here!"

"Give it a watch. Now, what is it you were gonna call me about?"

Zeke looked at me askance and waved a finger. "No, no. You tell me what you came in here for first. Let's get business out of the way."

I didn't have patience to play games with him, so I took a brown envelope out of my pocket and tossed it on the counter between us. It landed with the weight of a thick stack of twenty-dollar bills. I like to talk a lot about how cheap Ada is, but she never skimps on a bribe.

Zeke let out a low whistle, using one finger to open the end of the envelope and peek inside. "Who are you after this time? Bloodbag? Bone donor? Faust? I've got a lead on a guy in Columbus who supposedly owes Baron Samedi over thirty grand in Cuban cigars."

"Nah," I responded. "It's something a little different." I paused, looking up at the security camera blinking at me from one corner of the shop. "Turn that off."

"Eh? That's for my own personal safety, you know."

I laid one hand over the envelope of money. "Cameras off."

"Hold on, hold on." Zeke shuffled into the back room. The light on the camera went dead, and he returned a moment later carrying a salami sandwich. He took a bite and sat on a stool opposite me. "Lay it on thick, brother."

"I need discretion," I said.

"You know I'm the very model of discreet," Zeke replied, looking hurt.

"*Real* discretion," I repeated. I pulled another envelope out of my pocket and tossed it on top of the first. For a moment, I thought Zeke's eyes would pop out of his head.

"Frickin' A, Alek. You have my discretion," he said.

"Good. There's a *rumor* that a couple hundred souls have gone missing. I need to know if you've got a line on anything like that."

Zeke's eyes didn't leave the envelopes of money. He rubbed his chin. "Souls, huh? I've never heard of the Lords of Hell misplacing any of their gains. I didn't even know it could happen."

"So you haven't heard anything?"

"I'm not sure," he said, raising an eyebrow and flicking his eyes between my face and the money.

He's lying, Maggie told me. *He knows something, but I get the sense it's not that much.*

I shook my head at Zeke. "I'm not adding a penny to that pile unless you give me something really damn good."

Zeke's lips pursed stubbornly. "Whatever happened to some good, old-fashioned haggling?"

"I'm on a deadline," I told him.

For a fraction of a moment, I thought I saw the air around Zeke shimmer, and the vision of a tall, multiheaded, golden-skinned alien creature wafted behind him like a mirage. It was gone when I blinked, but I knew I had him. His disguise always wavered when he was about to relent.

"Okay," Zeke said, "I may have heard a thing or two. Nothing concrete, though. Just a tiny bit of hearsay."

"What kind of hearsay?" I asked.

Zeke said, "Supposedly there's this executive downtown who sold her soul for fame and power and all that. She paid her debt up front and has been living the high life ever since."

Paid her debt up front meant that she handed over her soul upon signature. *Most* people put off that part—they think if they keep their soul for twenty years then maybe the Devil will forget they exist or they'll be able to buy it back or something stupid. It's an easy negotiating point for my clients, so they let the sucker hold on to that soul and then don't pay nearly as much for it.

"What does this have to do with missing souls?" I asked.

"I'm getting there. *Supposedly*, she started to have her doubts about the whole heaven and hell thing last year, and get this..." Zeke paused dramatically. When I narrowed my eyes at his theatrics, he sighed and continued, "She bought herself a secondhand soul."

Now, that is very *interesting,* Maggie commented.

A little tickle went up my spine. "Secondhand souls aren't a thing," I said flatly.

Zeke shrugged. "That's what I thought. But when you mentioned missing souls, it popped into my head."

"What's the woman's name?"

"Can't help you there."

"Where did you hear this rumor?"

"Friend of a friend," Zeke said defensively. "You know I don't give up my sources."

He's told us all he knows, Maggie informed me.

I locked eyes with Zeke and took one of the envelopes back. I counted out two hundred dollars, threw the cash on the table, and put the envelope in my pocket.

"Hey, hey," Zeke said. "Come on!"

"You get to keep the envelope that shuts your mouth," I told him, "but that bit of info doesn't do much for me. You get me *more* info, and you might see the rest." I paused. "Unless you have something more to add. What was it you were going to call me about?

Zeke's frown passed, and he seemed uncertain. "It might be nothing."

"What kind of nothing?"

"There was this guy in here the other day asking after someone of your description."

"I'm a white guy with tattoos," I responded.

"Yeah, but he described your ring perfectly." He pointed at Maggie's ring.

Inside the back of my head, I felt Maggie become deathly still. I became suddenly self-conscious and resisted the urge to cover the ring with my hand. I'd never told a soul about the contents of the ring, and the only person who'd ever asked about it was Zeke. "What did he look like?" I asked.

"About five foot ten, black hair, black clothes. Emo type. I pegged him for an amateur necromancer. He smelled like black magic."

"You think he's dangerous?" I asked.

"Nothing you can't handle." Zeke chewed on his bottom lip. "But he's not the kind of guy I want to get the drop on you." I reached into my pocket, but Zeke held up both hands. "No charge for this one, buddy. I just wanted to warn you."

"I appreciate it." My mind was turning now, thinking over all the various debtors I'd dealt with the last couple years. The description didn't ring a bell, but that didn't mean some sour kid couldn't dye his hair and start dabbling in necromancy. It was the bit about Maggie's ring that worried me. "Did he ask after the ring itself, or just use it as part of the description he gave you?"

"Just the description."

Does this ring a bell? I asked Maggie.

No. Should it?

Any old enemies from before we met—or, hell, before you were trapped in there? Some of the Other live a damned long time.

Any enemies that still knew I was alive died centuries ago. I don't think I have any new enemies. It's kind of hard to piss people off from in here. She didn't sound all that worried, so I decided not to let it bother me.

"It's probably an old debtor," I told Zeke. "A lot of these assholes get mad when we take what they owe our clients. Instead of going after our clients, they go after us. Give me a call if he comes in here again, would you?"

"No problem."

He's not telling us everything, Maggie said.

Are you saying that because it's true, or because you don't like him?

Because it's true.

I eyed Zeke for a moment. He was as mercenary as they come, but I'd always been able to trust him as long as Ada kept paying for the information he gave us. We practically funded his gambling habit, after all. It was smart of him to keep us happy.

And I knew him well enough to see that he had told all he was going to tell.

"Thanks," I said again, turning toward the door.

"Hey," he asked, "this thing with the souls—who's the client on this, anyway? Lucy? If you see her, give her a peck on the cheek for me."

"Doesn't she still have a restraining order on you?"

"That's a misunderstanding," he replied with a pained look. "So who's the client?"

"You don't want to know," I said, heading toward the door.

"Oh, come on," Zeke said. "I'm already sworn to secrecy. Settle my curiosity." He searched the counter for a moment, and his face suddenly brightened up. "Hey, you tell me who the client is, and I'll hook you up with the next espresso machine that comes through here. Not one of those junk ones, either—a good one!"

I heard Maggie laugh in the back of my head. *Little bastard knows you too well.*

I considered for a moment. I *had* already bought his silence. "The client is Ferryman," I said, pushing open the door.

"Well, shiz," I heard him say as I left. "You weren't kidding. I really didn't want to know."

33

Chapter 4

A woman buying a secondhand soul might not sound like much to most people, but Zeke had given me enough information to get a serious start on this thing. First, I knew that she was a businesswoman working out of Cleveland. Second, I knew that she'd sold her soul at some point in the last two decades. If that was the case, I could track her down.

I called the office as I left Akron, waiting patiently until a woman's voice answered.

"Valkyrie Collections, this is Nadine. How may I help you?"

"Nadine, it's Alek."

"Oh, hey, hun! I saw you were here already this morning. I tell you, Alek, you don't have to make that shitty coffee. I'll bring you something good when I come in."

"I needed an early pick-me-up," I told her. Nadine is the reaper secretary. She's a heavyset black woman in her early fifties who hasn't missed a day of work for thirty years—other than the two weeks she takes off every December to go to the Caribbean. She prefers her nails long, her hair dyed, her designer clothes discounted, her shoes expensive, and her men confident. She's also the only person at Valkyrie who knows my true relationship with Ada, so she goes out of her way to make my life a little less miserable. She is, needless to say, one of my favorite people in the world.

"Well, you've got a chai latte sitting in the fridge with your name on it when you get back to the office, and I swear, if Karen tries to drink it, I will cut her."

"I appreciate it."

"Not a problem. Now, what can I do for you?"

"Did Ada tell you about the meeting with Ferryman this morning?"

Nadine snorted. "Yes, she did. That greasy old asshole left the whole office reeking of cigarettes. I've got a cleaning crew coming tomorrow to get the smell out before Ada gets back from Paris."

"Thanks for taking care of that. Ada has me working on Ferryman's job solo until it's finished, but I could use a little support help." Ferryman's request for discretion meant I couldn't depend on any of our normal skip tracers, but Nadine knew where *all* the bodies were buried in the company. I could trust her implicitly.

"Say the word."

"I need you to start calling all the minor soul collecting companies—our clients and anyone else you can think of—and tell them we're looking for a woman working out of downtown Cleveland who purchased wealth and power. The transaction was probably in the 2000s, but they should widen their search by a decade in each direction just in case."

"Mmmhmm. You do know the Lords of Hell don't like being asked questions about their clients, right?"

"Tell them the request comes straight from Ferryman and they can follow up with him if they aren't happy. We need the name of this woman."

"I'll give it a go," she promised. "This might take a couple of days. Half those pricks don't answer their phones."

"Whatever it takes. I'll start with our big seven right now, so don't worry about them."

"Understood. Good luck."

I stopped at the next Starbucks and charged a cappuccino to the company credit card before claiming a corner table and setting my phone on the table in front of me.

You think they'll actually answer your questions? Maggie asked. *Nadine was right—they hate talking about their clients.*

They will if they want to find their missing souls, I told her, and started my first call.

I spent the next several hours talking to what felt like every secretary in Hell. Lucy was in meetings all day. Satan's people told me they didn't have any Cleveland execs in their records. Modius claimed they didn't do business in Midwest, though I knew for a fact that they did. ViaTech, Leviathan Industries, and BeelzMart all came up with nothing. Mammon hadn't been in the soul business for centuries, so I didn't bother calling him. And—no surprise—Belphagor wouldn't answer his goddamn phone.

I finally hung up after trying to get through to somebody at LuciCorp who could give me a straight answer and rubbed the gums below my bottom canines. I had no word from Nadine, which meant she hadn't gotten any further than I had.

Any idea what you'll do if this is a dud? Maggie asked. She'd been quiet since I'd started my calls—probably reading a book or something.

I shook my head. It was something I hadn't had time to consider. *I'll start hitting the rest of my contacts and see what I can drum up.* I'd begun with Zeke because he came through the most often with me, and despite his mercenary behavior, he wouldn't say a word about my investigation to anyone once he'd been paid. I couldn't say the same thing about most of the other snitches in town. *If we can't come up with a solid lead, I'll go back to Ferryman and press him for more information. He held back something. If I need to, I'll make sure he tells me what.*

Maggie laughed. *You've got balls; I'll give you that. If I ever meet Death, it's gonna be all, "yes, sir," and "no, sir," for me.*

You did meet him, I pointed out. *He just didn't know you were there.*

I got up and ordered another cappuccino, then returned to my seat and watched as the last of the lunchtime stragglers finished their coffees and headed back to their offices or gyms or homes or wherever people go during the middle of the day. I spun my phone on the table with one finger and tried not to think about how long this week would be if I couldn't track down Ferryman's thieves quickly. It wasn't just that I wanted to finish the job—I wanted to get free of Ada for a few days so that Maggie could enjoy her anniversary. And I damn well needed a break too.

Heads up, came a whisper from Maggie.

Huh?

Something's not right.

I raised my head and looked around the Starbucks. Other than me and one lady in the opposite corner, the place was empty. Two workers cleaned equipment behind the glass case of snacks.

The black Caddie that just pulled in to the parking lot, Maggie said.

I leaned back to get a good look out the window. A black Cadillac had, indeed, just pulled into the parking lot. Three people got out. One of them did a circuit around my truck, then all three headed toward the front door of the Starbucks.

Two of them looked like identical twins. They were tall—easily six foot six—and gaunt, wearing sunglasses, baseball caps, hoodies, and jeans. The third was maybe five foot eight, wearing a black sports jacket over a black T-shirt with black slacks and slicked-back black hair. He was clean-shaven and baby faced, and he wore a scowl that gave me the impression that he wanted to look tough.

I think that Zeke's amateur necromancer just found us, I told Maggie. *How the hell did he figure out where I was?*

Beats me. Keep your guard up. That kid looks like a piece of shit, but he's got some serious raw power. And I can't read his two spooks at all.

I pushed my chair back from the table and slid my notes into the bag beneath my seat, adopting a casual pose as I sipped my drink. The trio entered, looked around once, and headed straight for me. The amateur necromancer slid into the chair across the table from me, while his companions took up positions to block my escape route to the door.

I ignored the kid for a moment and gave the big guys a quick up and down. This close, I could see cracked, sallow skin and fingernails blackened with age. They stood unnaturally, stiff and unresponsive like the model of a skeleton in the corner of a doctor's office. *No wonder you can't get a read on them,* I told Maggie. *They're fucking draugr.* Undead are always a little tricky to detect with sorcery. They occupy a place between our world and the next in a way that gives them a sort of false sorcerous aura.

What kind of prick brings draugr out in broad daylight? Maggie demanded.

Hold on; I'll ask.

I turned my attention to kid sitting across from me and fixed him with my best annoyed stare. "What kind of a prick brings two draugr out in broad daylight?" I asked.

The kid opened his mouth, closed it again, and scowled. "Give me the location of your jinn, and this doesn't have to get unpleasant."

Give him what? Maggie asked.

"Give you what?" I said aloud at the same time. My mind suddenly kicked into overdrive, and I felt myself tense involuntarily. Not a soul in the world knew that I had a jinn ring on my finger. Maggie might have been trapped in there, but she still had access to no small amount of power, which she used to keep herself hidden. She wanted to keep from falling into the wrong hands almost as much as I wanted to keep people from knowing I had an ace up my sleeve.

"The jinn," the kid repeated. "Don't play coy. I know that you have the vessel containing Margarete Abaroa. It is not your property, and I've been tasked with returning it to the proper owner." His scowl disappeared into a businesslike look of disdain.

He certainly knows how to play it cool, I told Maggie.

He's an asshole, Maggie snarled. *My ring is no one's property but my own.*

I was taken aback at the anger in her voice. Maggie was not prone to hysterics, so for her to become genuinely furious about something took some doing. Of course, I don't like it when people upset my friends.

I gave the two draugr a sidelong glance. "I don't know what you're talking about. A jinn? Where would I even keep such a thing?"

The kid seemed to take my question literally. "Traditionally in a lamp, but other vessels have been known. Rings are popular." His gaze flicked to Maggie's ring, but nothing about his posture told me he knew that I had her with me right now. "You can hand it over," he continued, "or tell me where it is. Otherwise, I'll be forced to kill you and reanimate your corpse so *it* can tell me where to find the jinn. I would prefer you make your decision quickly. I don't have all day."

I opened my mouth to respond, but he cut me off.

"Don't try to run. You seem to already know what the gentlemen beside you are, so…"

I cut him off in turn. "Yeah, I know what a draugr is, buddy. And look, I'm crazy amounts of impressed that you've managed to raise *and* keep control of them. In broad daylight, no less. But this is a Starbucks in a crowded city. It's the worst possible place to kill a dude."

A hint of uncertainty crossed the kid's face. "If you choose to be difficult, you will forfeit the lives of everyone in this shop. I will not leave witnesses."

Okay, I told Maggie, *he's getting on my nerves.*

I need answers, she responded sharply.

It was the closest to a command that I'd ever gotten from Maggie, and it kind of annoyed me. "We should establish something really quick," I said, holding up a finger at the kid.

The necromancer licked his lips. He had a nervous glint in his eye, like he'd finally realized that if I knew what a draugr was and wasn't reacting with fear, he might be in trouble. "What?" he demanded.

"Do you know who I am? Not, like, in a pretentious way. I'm just curious if you know who I am or what I do for a living."

"I don't care. All I know is that you carry the jinn. That's all I need to know."

Is he powerful enough to be this arrogant? I asked Maggie.

Powerful enough? Sure. But he can't be more than nineteen, so he probably doesn't have the chops to use his power.

Him first, then.

"Let's start with names," I said. "I'm Alek." Reaching across the table, I snatched him by the hair and slammed his face into the tabletop.

The draugr moved fast enough that one snatched me by the arm the moment its master's head hit the table. With a quick motion, it planted its feet, grabbed me by the shoulder, and yanked. Draugr are *strong*, and if I were fully human, it would have ripped my arm off entirely. As it was, I let out an undignified gasp as I felt my arm get pulled out of its socket.

My bottom canines transformed almost instantly, turning into thumb-sized tusks that ripped painfully through my gums and jutted from my lower jaw. The troll berserker in me took over, and I was out of the chair in the blink of an eye. The tattoo of Mjolnir flared to life on my right fist, glowing like the embers of a fire, and I slammed it into the draugr's stomach hard enough to rip through the desiccated, sorcery-strengthened skin and out the other side.

I took a punch from the other draugr, which sent me staggering into a chair and going down in a heap with the fellow I was now wearing as a bracelet. Someone in the building screamed. I landed hard, rolled on top of the undead, and pulled out its willowy spine. The creature dissolved into dust beneath me.

The second draugr grabbed me by the shoulders and squeezed. I could feel its powerful fingers begin to push through my skin, and I groaned at the pain. I got to one knee, grappling the creature around the middle and lifting it off the ground. I took us both across the middle of the Starbucks. Draugr first, we went through the glass snack case and tumbled into the prep area.

The draugr's sunglasses were knocked off, and I stared into empty pits that had once housed eyes. It howled at me angrily, thrashing, and wrapped one bony hand around my left wrist. I punched the creature in the head, my Mjolnir tattoo giving off tiny sparks of sorcery. Its neck snapped back, and it howled at it me again. Reaching up, I grabbed an espresso machine and pulled it down onto the creature's chest.

The damn thing finally let go of my wrist. It struggled, trying to push the machine off it, and I got to my feet and brought a boot down on the creature's forehead—again and again. Bone crunched under my heel, and the body finally dissolved in the same way the first one had.

I staggered back, wiped my forehead, and noticed that the employees were cowering in the back room, watching me with eyes wide. "Give me a minute, then call 911," I told them.

I stepped through the shattered snack case and walked over to the necromancer. The blow I'd given him had put him out cold, but he was beginning to come around. I lifted him by the back of the neck and put him on the ground, rubbing his face in the dust of his draugr, then flipped him over so I could see his eyes.

Tell me if he tries anything, I said to Maggie.

I slapped him until he began to sputter. "What's your name?" I asked.

"It's Nick, damn it! Stop hitting me!"

"Nick the Necromancer. That's adorable." I slapped him again, then grasped him by the chin. My tusks were still out, and I didn't bother to force them to retract. His eyes widened at the sight of them. "Look, Nick, you asshole, you don't bring draugr into a Starbucks on a Saturday afternoon. Demigods don't pull that kind of shit! There are Rules. Who the hell do you think you are?"

"I'll show you who I am," he growled.

He's going to try and cast some kind of decaying spell on you, Maggie warned.

I broke two fingers on his right hand. *That should keep him distracted.* I let him scream for a few seconds. "All right, Nick, tell me who sent you after me."

"Go to hell," he gasped.

I rolled my eyes. "I'm not gonna sit here and torture you all day, Nick. I work for a living. Tell me who you are, or I call OtherOps."

He just stared at me balefully, so I got up and shouted to the employees. "Call 911. Tell them a necromancer and two draugr just jumped a reaper agent. They'll patch you through to the right place."

"You're a reaper?"

I looked back down at Nick. The cold, calculating necromancer was gone, and in his place was a nineteen-year-old kid who knew he'd just fucked up—big time. "Yup. I deal with shit like this all the time. Whoever hired you either had no idea who I am or threw you straight to the wolves. Gonna tell me a name?"

He frowned, and I could see in his eyes that he considered it a moment before shaking his head.

"At least tell me how you found me," I said. "Do you have a tracker on my car?"

He hesitated for a moment before speaking. "Zeke called me when you arrived at his place this morning. I followed you from the pawnshop, and I've been watching you for the last couple of hours."

"Zeke, you greedy piece of shit," I muttered to myself.

I tried to warn you about him, Maggie said.

Oddly enough, I couldn't summon any real anger. This

kind of shit was in Zeke's nature. It would be like getting mad at a dog for eating the bagel you dropped on the floor. *Eh, he did warn me,* I told Maggie. *And he knew I would be able to handle the kid.* "See, that wasn't too hard, was it?" I said to Nick. "You can make this easier and tell me the name of whoever hired you. I might even forget to press charges."

Nick remained silent.

Let me at him, Maggie whispered in the back of my head.

No.

What do you mean, "no"?

I mean no. I can feel how pissed you are right now. If I touch him with your ring, you'll kill him.

Maggie muttered to herself angrily. I ignored her, put my boot on Nick's chest, and waited for OtherOps to arrive.

"And you're sure you've never seen him before in your life?"

"Never," I assured the OtherOps agent who stood beside me in front of the Starbucks. I watched over his shoulder as Nick was loaded into the back of an OtherOps paddy wagon. The OtherOps agent was a middle-aged bureaucratic type, yawning at the destruction caused by the draugr, pen poised above his notepad.

"He claims you have some sort of property of his," the agent said, "but he wouldn't elaborate further. Do you want to comment on that?"

So Nick hadn't told OtherOps what he was after. That shouldn't surprise me. If this was a legit recovery, I would have been confronted by the cops and not some punk necromancer mercenary. I let my eyes wander back to the agent, then down to his name tag. "Agent Lindberg, I have absolutely no idea what that asshole is talking about. I've dealt with a lot of nutters in my job, and he's just about as crazy as they come."

"He seems pretty sane to me."

"Draugr in a Starbucks, Lindberg. That's all I have to say."

The average person might have an inkling that the Other existed, but nobody actually wanted to *think* about how closely our two worlds overlapped. For centuries, the Rules have kept most of this sort of stuff out of the public eye. Nick was going to find himself in trouble with both the humans and the Other. It wasn't going to go well for him.

Agent Lindberg gave a snort and flipped his notebook shut. "All right, you're free to go. If you think of any reason at all why this man would attack you, give me a call." He handed me his card, which I pocketed. The agent headed inside, where a team worked on cleaning the draugr dust from the crime scene. Some lady in a suit stood nearby, yapping into a cell phone—probably someone from Starbucks corporate talking to their insurance. A couple of plainclothes OtherOps agents spoke quietly with the Starbucks employees. They'd probably get a small payout and pro bono counseling for their proximity to the incident.

I rubbed my torn-up gums. I heal a little faster than normal humans, but they would hurt for days. My tusks were gone and my tattoos had stopped glowing, but I had a good ache in my jaw and shoulders from the fight. I'd managed to pop my arm back into its socket before OtherOps arrived, but that hurt too.

Maggie? I said tentatively, getting into my truck.

No response. I could feel her presence in the ring.

Come on.

Hmph, she responded.

I wasn't gonna let you kill that kid.

He would have told me who he worked for.

Maybe, maybe not. I've got friends at OtherOps. Once he's stewed in a cell for a few days, we'll see if he wants to talk. No killing needed.

She scoffed. *He tried to kill you first. Why are you sticking up for him?*

Because he's still a teenager. I can't even imagine being a hormonal prick and *having the powers of a necromancer. If he were some grizzled old vet, sure. But he's still a kid.*

He'll come after you when he gets out.

If he does, you can say you told me so as one of his draugr chokes the life out of me. Maggie didn't respond, and I could sense that something was different about her brooding. *What is it?* I asked.

This isn't a joke, Alek. Someone knows I'm alive. They know I'm trapped in here. And they know you carry my ring. I'm not sure how to stress to you how big a deal that is.

I mulled over the thought for a moment. She'd been trapped in there for over five hundred years, and she'd only spent about ten years of that with me. There was a lot of background that I had no context for, but I had no reason to disbelieve her. *Look, I know you don't like to talk about your past, but since I'm the one facing whoever decides to come after you, I really need to know who or what that might be. So if you have anything you're holding back…*

I'm not. I'd expected her to sound indignant at my accusation, but she seemed more frustrated than anything else. *I've been wracking my mind for who I might have pissed off that's still hanging around, and I can't think of anyone. I haven't walked the Earth as free jinn for a really long time. And that narrows down the list to immortals and very long-lived Others.*

Okay. Let's let the kid stew for a couple days, then we'll work him over. We'll find out who hired him and go after that person once we're finished with Ferryman's job.

Promise?

Promise. Hell, maybe we can spend your anniversary tracking down an old enemy of yours.

Chapter 5

I got a phone call from a blocked number on my way to work Monday morning. "Alek Fitz," I answered groggily.

"How's my little Norseman this morning?" It was one of those voices that that immediately made you imagine a full pair of pouty lips. A little tickle went up the side of my neck, as if the owner of those lips had blown gently on that sensitive spot just beneath my ear. It was a voice that demanded attention. All traces of sleepiness disappeared.

"Hi, Lucy," I said warmly. "You think you could have called me back last night?"

Lucy—or Lucifer, to use her given name—is my favorite client. She's the CEO of LuciCorp and the most well-known of the Lords of Hell. I like Lucy a lot, and I've always felt like she gets a historically bad rap. She's a top-notch businesswoman, sends me gift baskets every Christmas, and has a great sense of humor.

I heard a scoff from the other end of the line. "Always business with you, isn't it? I was stuck in an orgy until almost two. You don't want me to call at two, do you?"

"Not unless you're inviting me along."

A wicked laugh responded. "You know you're always welcome."

I sucked on my teeth, rolled my eyes, and thought of velvet cushions and top-shelf liquor. I felt a presence stir in Maggie's ring. "The last time I went to one of your parties, I could barely see for six weeks."

"And it was completely worth it, wasn't it?"

You'd better say yes, Maggie said. *That party was the most fun I've had in centuries, and I only got to watch.*

"You know I work for a living, don't you?" I asked Lucy.

"Pishposh. I'll lean on Ada—have her send you out here

for a consultation of some sort. I seem to remember there being a very cute little fire demon that you got to know pretty well."

Oh, I remember her, Maggie said.

I felt my cheeks warm. I remembered her too. Occasionally—just occasionally—I love my job. "I got to know a lot of people," I told Lucy. "It's all a little hazy. How about you give me a hand now, and we can talk about parties next time, eh? I'm looking for a lady who sold her soul in Cleveland. High-powered exec of some sort."

"My secretary told me." Lucy's voice switched from flirtatious to all business without missing a beat. "She's not an exec; she's a lawyer. Normally I wouldn't give out this sort of information, but I'm told this has to do with the little issue that Ferryman is dealing with."

"That's right."

"Her name is Judith Pyke. She's a partner at the law firm Wilson and Pyke. I'll email over all the info we have on her."

"I really appreciate it."

"Anything for you, troll boy." Her voice slid back to flirtatious. "Oh, and tell Nadine to answer my texts. I have board meetings all afternoon, and I need something to keep me occupied."

"Uh," I said, "since when do you text with Nadine?"

"Are you joking? Nadine is the funniest person I know in the entire Midwest. We've been going on holiday together for years."

"You think you know a person," I muttered to myself, pulling into the Valkyrie Collections parking lot. My phone beeped, indicating an incoming call. "I've got to go. Send me the information, and let me know when you're in town next. We'll get dinner and charge it to Ada's credit card."

"I like the way you think." The line went dead, and I switched over. "Alek Fitz."

"Do you have any good news for me?" It was Ada.

I swore silently. I should have let it go to voicemail and claimed ignorance later. "Nothing yet," I told her. There was a long, disapproving silence. I rolled my eyes and tried not to panic as the barcode on my chest tightened. "Look," I continued, "it's been two days. I worked all weekend despite some asshole necromancer jumping me at Starbucks."

Ada sniffed. My barcode continued to feel progressively more uncomfortable. "Ah, yes. What was that about, anyway?"

"No idea," I lied. "He won't tell me, and he won't tell OtherOps. Probably an old debtor coming back for revenge." My breathing began to feel restricted, and I silently cursed Ada. "I'm hitting the pavement hard on this Ferryman business. I just talked to Lucy. She's sending me some info that I'm going to check out this morning."

The tightness disappeared, and I took a deep breath to hold in an angry growl.

"Fine," Ada said. "Just don't goof off. We don't get the chance to impress someone like Ferryman too often." She hung up.

"Goof off," I muttered, rubbing my bar code. "Since when do I goof off?" I sat in the car for a few minutes while I waited for Lucy to send over Judith Pyke's information. Once I had it, I went inside, said good morning to Nadine—and told her to return Lucy's texts—then headed straight back out on the road to downtown.

Judith's office was in 200 Public Square, one of the big skyscrapers downtown. I parked in a nearby garage, where I checked for security cameras before changing quickly into a shirt that I kept carefully folded in a bag beneath my driver's seat. It was a black button-down shirt with a white diagonal stripe across the front and the word OTHEROPS emblazoned over the left breast. I could hear Maggie humming to herself as I changed.

You enjoy this far too much, I told her.

Oh, come on. You know I love it when you impersonate an OtherOps agent.

I really shouldn't, I replied. *If I run into an actual OtherOps agent, I'm screwed.* I could practically see Maggie grinning at the idea. I could never quite decide whether she enjoyed watching me play dress up or just got a thrill from the danger of it. Probably a mix of both. *You know, if they catch me, they'll confiscate your ring. Or at least they'll try to. That's what cops do.*

The humming stopped.

I walked in through the front door, wearing a black, nondescript windbreaker over my OtherOps shirt, and headed across the big atrium, where I checked in with the front desk using a fake ID. I was soon on my way up to the law offices of Wilson and Pyke. I got off the elevator on the seventeenth floor, where I went through a series of hallways before finding myself in a small reception area with frosted glass walls and a single secretary's desk.

The secretary was a clean-shaven, immaculately professional young man with dark hair and severe eyebrows who sat straight-backed in his chair. He fixed me with that hollow secretary smile and tilted his head condescendingly to one side. "Good morning, sir. May I help you?"

"I'm looking for Mrs. Pyke," I responded. I pulled a business card out of the breast pocket of my OtherOps shirt. It had a fake name on it and a phone number and email address that forwarded to my real ones.

"Do you have an appointment?"

"No," I said. "Please call her office and let her know that Agent Gee from OtherOps is here to see her."

The secretary examined my card for a moment. "I'm sorry, but *Miss* Pyke isn't in right now."

He's lying, Maggie said.

"Fine," I told him, keeping straight-faced. "When will she be back? I'll wait inside."

"I'm afraid I can't let you in the office without a warrant,

Mr. Gee."

"*Agent* Gee." I fixed him with my best withering look. "Sir, I'll be frank: you must be new here, because if you weren't, you'd know that OtherOps doesn't work like regular police. This isn't an antagonistic visit. Just get your damn boss on the phone."

Oh, I love it when you do your official business voice, Maggie whispered.

I had to bite my cheek to keep from cracking a smile. I unzipped my windbreaker so that he could see the shirt and official-looking lanyard beneath it. The secretary eyed me warily for a moment before picking up the phone. "She's with a client right now, but she should be almost done. Hold on a moment while I check."

I did a circuit of the little reception room while I waited. It was stylish but empty, with industrial-grade carpet to give it a warmer feeling, tall ceilings, gold fixtures, and those frosted glass walls to give you the impression that VERY IMPORTANT THINGS were happening just beyond that door. *I can't get anything from inside,* Maggie told me. *Damned law offices love to ward up super tight. But it means they've got some serious capital.*

The woman sold her soul to LuciCorp. I sure hope *she has serious capital.*

Our brief conversation was interrupted by the secretary clearing his throat. I returned my attention to the man, only to find him fixed with a look of consternation.

Something is wrong, Maggie said.

I gathered as much.

I approached the desk slowly. The secretary's face was white, and he trembled slightly. "Uh, you're a cop, right?"

"Kind of," I replied cautiously.

"Because Miss Pyke just gave me the code word to call the police on the gentlemen she's meeting with."

"Shit," I said, moving quickly toward the door. "What am

I dealing with? Who is she meeting?"

"I'm not sure! She said they were clients. It's a group of imps; I…"

Imps. Of course it had to be imps. I didn't wait for him to finish and hit the door running. As soon as I was inside the actual office, I heard Maggie let out a soft gasp. *I'm in,* she said.

Talk to me!

Head to the end of the hall and take a right. Corner office. Five imps. One standing guard, four in there with her. They're armed. As she spoke, I produced my Glock from my endless wallet, then a little black cylinder that I screwed onto the end. It looked an awful lot like the type of silencer you see in the movies, but unlike those, this one was wrapped in black magic and actually worked like everyone *thinks* real silencers work. I was not, after all, a real OtherOps agent. I didn't want to attract attention.

The office is empty except for Judith and the secretary, Maggie told me.

Good. I rounded the corner at a sprint and caught sight of a short, ugly man in a cheap black suit standing outside the door to the corner office, his attention on his phone. "OtherOps! Hands where I can see them!" I bellowed.

The imp nearly leapt out of his skin. He swung toward me, his mouth opening in surprise, which quickly changed to a snarl. He reached into his jacket. I squeezed the trigger twice without a second thought. The magical silencer made a high-pitched sound, tinkling like broken glass, and both shots took him in the chest, spinning him around before he dropped to the floor. I reached Judith's door and set my feet, putting my shoulder into it hard enough to burst straight through the wood and into a room where all activity seemed to freeze upon my arrival.

I stood in a large executive office with a glass desk opposite a leather couch. An imp sat behind the desk playing with a bunch of paper clips. A second and third imp held a middle-aged woman down on the couch while a fourth stood over her face holding a soul mirror. All of them looked up at me, mouths open.

These fuckers are dangerous, Maggie said. *Put 'em down so they don't get back up.*

She didn't have to tell me twice.

Everyone moved at once. The three imps with Judith leapt to their feet. I took out the one with the soul mirror with three shots and the friend closest to him with another two. The third leapt at me with a scream, and I caught him by the throat with my left hand. I felt a flare of sorcery from Maggie's ring, and the imp's head burst into a smokeless flame so hot I had to throw him away. The last imp came out of the desk chair, gun in hand, and went down with three more shots.

I froze, my eyes moving around the office and blood pounding in my ears. The whole thing had happened so quickly that I could still feel my tusks growing in reaction to the adrenaline. I forced them to retract, rubbing my gums with my left hand and trying to blink through the daze brought on by such sudden violence.

I checked the imp just outside the door, then did a quick circuit of the other three I'd shot. Every one of them was dead, or would be within a few minutes. I didn't even bother checking for a pulse on the one Maggie had gotten her claws into. He lay in the corner, his bare skull smoldering through the end of his unintended Ghost Rider impression. Thankfully, the sorcerous flames hadn't lit the carpet.

I headed to the couch to get my first look at Judith Pyke. Judith, it seemed, had seen better days. She was deathly pale, her body emaciated and frail. She looked like she could barely stand, let alone fight off a group of imps. She lay still, her eyes open and her breath wheezy as she stared at the bodies scattered around the room.

Jesus, Maggie whispered. *She's rotting from the inside out. For real?*

Yeah. I've never sensed anything like it. I could hear the revulsion in Maggie's voice.

"Miss Pyke," I said gently, "are you okay?"

She trembled, her eyes continuing to move from imp corpse to imp corpse before finally settling on my face. She managed the barest hint of a nod. I heard a noise beyond me and turned quickly to find the secretary standing in the doorway, his eyes wide. "Were there only five of them?" I asked, even though Maggie had already given me that answer.

"Ye... ye... yes," the secretary stammered. "Sh... sh... should I call the cops?"

"I am the cops, remember? Don't call anyone." The last thing I needed was the real OtherOps showing up to ask questions. "Has she always looked like this?"

"No, sir. Only for a few months or so. She's been going to doctors, but no one seems to know what's wrong."

I already had a sneaking suspicion that *I* knew what was wrong, the same way a mechanic can tell when a clunky engine has been fixed with substandard parts. "Ma'am," I said in a low voice to Judith, "did you purchase a secondhand soul?"

Another barely perceptible nod.

Has she been sedated? I asked Maggie.

Not as far as I can tell. This is all her.

I did another circuit around the room and found the soul mirror that had been dropped by one of the imps. It looked like my own standard-issue gear—equipment procured directly from the soul dealers. I put it in my pocket, then opened up my wallet to find one of my own. Most soul mirrors had fingerprints on them—mirrors waiting to be used on debtors—but I was able to dig up a blank one. I sat down on the sofa beside Judith. "I've got to get it out of you," I told her. "I'm sorry." Moving quickly, I used two fingers to hold open her right eye and held the mirror above it. She shuddered once, and the mirror warmed to my touch. When I took it away, her eyes were closed.

I checked her pulse.

"Is she going to be okay?" the secretary asked. He still stood in the doorway, wringing his hands, studiously avoiding looking at the corpses.

"Of course she is," I told him. In truth, I had no idea. I'd never seen anything like this before. Maggie mentioned a rot. If it was caused by the secondhand soul, there was no telling what kind of side effects might remain. *Any idea if she's going to wake up soon?* I asked Maggie.

I can't tell. Her heartbeat is regular, and she's still breathing.

If she doesn't wake up...

You'll be in deep shit?

I was going to say that I'd feel terrible if I killed her with a soul mirror, but yeah, I'd also be in deep shit.

I looked at the secretary. "Go back to your desk. I'm going to make some phone calls and get the proper people here to deal with the bodies. If anyone comes to the office asking questions, get rid of them. And don't call anyone, not even her partner." Once the secretary had withdrawn, I took out my phone and dialed Ferryman's answering service.

"Hello. This is Alek Fitz. Tell Ferryman that I need five bodies gotten rid of quietly and quickly. Yes, I'll wait for a call back."

I hung up, turned on my camera app, and began to take pictures of the dead imps.

Much to my surprise, Judith was sitting up within half an hour. She stared despondently at the bloodstains on the carpet, her eyes avoiding the pile of imps I'd stacked neatly in one corner and covered with a blanket from the sofa. Even in such a short time, she already looked improved; some of the color had returned to her face, and she seemed to be able to move—if painfully—under her own power. Her secretary brought her a cup of coffee, then retreated, after which Judith returned her gaze to me.

"Why are you pretending to be an OtherOps agent?" she asked.

I'd already introduced myself for real, and I gave her a tight smile at the question. "If I'd shown up and told the secretary I was a reaper, you wouldn't have seen me."

"Why do you think that?"

"Because you'd assume I was either here for a client or for the secondhand soul. You wouldn't have wanted to talk to me about either. Reapers might have some pull, but nobody says no to OtherOps."

She sniffed, took a sip of her coffee, and then held it in both hands to hide their trembling. Despite her condition, she still had sharp eyes, and she managed a stern, disaffected air. "You're not wrong. I suppose I shouldn't report you, considering the circumstances."

I heard Maggie laugh in the back of my head. *She's an arrogant old broad. Should you point out that if she reports you she'll go down for soul fraud?*

I don't think that's a thing, I told her.

It will be if she calls OtherOps on you.

"I appreciate that," I said to Judith. "This secondhand soul—what can you tell me about it?"

She hesitated before answering. "I've suspected that it was killing me since I first got it."

"And how long have you had the soul?"

"Four months or so."

"And how long until it started to do this to you?" I asked, gesturing at her emaciated body.

Judith shook her head. "I started to feel strange within a week. The physical changes became apparent after a month."

"If you suspected something was wrong, why didn't

you just call the guy you bought it from and ask to have it removed?"

Judith rasped a chuckle. "Denial, I suppose. I wanted to believe I was just sick. Do you know what it's like to not have your soul?"

"I wouldn't, no." A better reaper might have injected a little sympathy into their voice. With my background, I have a hard time relating to anyone who willingly makes deals with the Other. "But I've heard it starts to hurt after a while."

"Not hurt," Judith explained. "Not exactly. You just start to feel... empty. Like a shell. It's like a really bad breakup, where no amount of joy can fill the void left behind. Nothing—money, food, sex, power, thrill. Life becomes tasteless. I sold out to LuciCorp fifteen years ago. I paid immediately. None of those damned deferment plans that eventually find the reapers at your door. It took almost a decade for the emptiness to hit. After a while, it was all I could think about. Then..." She gestured to the pile of dead imps. "One of these little bastards showed up at the office and offered to sell me a used soul. Claimed it would feel just like my old one, and I'd be back to normal within weeks."

"How much did you pay?" I asked.

"Five hundred grand."

Maggie let out a low whistle.

I said, "I'm looking for the people who sold this to you. Did I get them all?" I certainly hoped not. If I had, I'd just killed everyone who could tell me where to find the rest of Ferryman's missing souls. I was pretty sure I was in the clear, though. Imps rarely act on their own.

"No, no," Judith answered. "At least, I don't think so. I don't actually recognize any of those... gentlemen. I only let them in because one knew that I was sick and claimed he could help me." She scowled into the distance, her eyes hopeless. "They were going to kill me."

That was interesting. "How do you know?" I asked.

"They talked about it. I could barely fight back. They said they were going to repossess the soul they sold me, then slit my throat. They would have killed Robert, too—gotten rid of us and then sold the soul to the next poor sap."

I assumed Robert was her secretary. "Imps are gossips," I told her, "and they're savage little bastards who tend to be low on the food chain. Whenever they get a chance to lord over others, they do. Do you know who their boss is?"

Judith shook her head. "I paid in cash. Dropped it off at a warehouse in the Flats." She tried to get up, and I had to help her to her feet. She teetered over to a filing cabinet and came back with a scrap of paper. "That address." She leaned heavily against the wall, staring at the covered corpses, and I thought I saw a flicker of life—of anger—in her eyes. "I'm going to leave town for a while."

"Probably a good idea," I answered. "People will be here to clean all this up in ten minutes. You'll want to make sure that your secretary—Robert, was it?"

"Yes."

"That Robert doesn't tell anyone about this. It's best if he keeps thinking I'm OtherOps, but if OtherOps does show up for some reason... well, I was never here."

"I understand."

"Good." I felt around my lower canines with my tongue. I could still taste some blood from where they'd split the gums. It was painful, but a good kind of pain. The berserker in me enjoyed the sight of the bodies in the corner, relishing the memory of putting down five of those creepy little fuckwits. The human part of me felt vaguely ill. I'm a good reaper partially because I'm dangerous, yes, but I'm not an assassin or a thug. Without Maggie's urging and that troll blood in my veins, I would have moved a little more cautiously—maybe even left an imp alive for Maggie to question. I felt foolish.

I exchanged cards with Judith and stepped outside just in time to see Ferryman's cleanup squad enter the office. There were over a dozen of them—all human, as far as I could tell, and the group included janitors, a butcher, carpet men, and even a couple of guys wearing the shirts of a local glass company, here to replace the one frosted glass wall I'd shot out in my little rampage. I stepped around them and headed into the hallway, where I wished, not for the first time, that I followed in the footsteps of almost everyone else at Valkyrie and smoked. It might have relieved some of my tension.

You don't seem too hot right now, Maggie said.

I just killed five people.

Imps.

Yeah, imps. They're not human, but I'd still feel bad if I hit a dog with my car. Besides, I should have left one alive.

Move too slowly, and that one might have gotten the drop on you.

I snorted. She was right, of course. Always shoot first and ask questions later when it comes to a room full of hostile imps. But I still didn't feel great about it. *I'm taking the rest of the day off. I'll call a friend of mine at OtherOps and find out who owns this warehouse. Then we'll hit it first thing in the morning.*

Chapter 6

The warehouse at the address Judith gave me was empty.

I stood just inside the open door of a truck loading bay and gazed across thirty thousand square feet of breezy concrete lit by morning sunlight streaming in through broken pane windows near the ceiling. Taking a quick walk around the open space, I found a bit of trash, plenty of dust, and no evidence that anything of substance had been stored here for some time. I returned to my truck and dialed Judith, who picked up on the second ring.

"I'm at the address you gave me," I told her. "When you dropped off the money here, did you actually go inside?"

"I did."

"Was the warehouse being used for anything?"

"I'm not sure. I just went up to the office on the left."

I spotted a small staircase off to one side of the truck loading bay. It led to a windowless manager's door. "Hold on for a moment, please," I told her. I ran up the stairs and tried the knob. It was unlocked. I flipped on the lights. The room inside was just as empty as the warehouse. "Any other details you can remember?" I asked Judith.

"I gave them the money. They used one of those mirrors to give me that damn soul, and I left. I think there were three or four imps inside having lunch at the time. There really isn't anything else."

That's all she knows, Maggie confirmed in the back of my head.

"Understood. Thank you."

I hung up and called my friend at OtherOps. Justin and I go back longer than me and Maggie. I like to call him a desk jockey because he hates leaving the office, but he was a capable agent and third in command at the Cleveland

OtherOps office. My call went to voicemail, but he rang back almost the instant I hung up the phone.

"Alek," he said, "you get anything at that warehouse?"

"Nothing. Everything is unlocked, and the place is empty."

He snorted and said, "I got in touch with the owner this morning. Turns out she rents to anybody willing to pay cash up front, no questions asked. Her last tenant was human, but she doesn't have much of a description: male, six feet, blond hair."

"That could be me," I said flatly.

"Yeah, she wasn't very helpful. She *did* say that they still have three months prepaid on the rent. Someone was there, but it sounds like they cleared out before you could reach them."

Human, huh? Maggie said. *So the imps definitely aren't working alone.*

Sure sounds like it. We just need to find out if this human is another henchman or the big boss.

You make it sound like a video game.

Don't shit on the ways I keep my life interesting, I told her.

I said to Justin, "Any word on who hired that necromancer to rough me up?"

"Nothing," Justin replied. "The kid won't say a damn word to anyone at the station. I've got our sorcery specialist talking to him right now. Hopefully I'll get a little more out of him at some point."

"I appreciate it."

There was a pause from the other end of the line. "You, uh, gonna tell me who you're after this time? Is it teeth? You're always chasing teeth."

"I don't actually do that many teeth these days. The Tooth Fairy is semiretired, and Jinn Enterprises has scaled back their Midwest operations."

"Blood?"

"Nope."

"So are you going to tell me?"

"Sorry, client confidentiality. But I'll buy you a beer next week if you've got the time."

"Deal."

I hung up and stared at the warehouse, feeling more than a little annoyed. Ferryman was wrong about one thing: that souls didn't have any value in this life. Judith had paid half a million for that secondhand shit. I had plenty of smoke—five dead imps and a half-dead lawyer—but no actual fire. Someone in town was running a very lucrative scam with Ferryman's missing souls, and if Judith's run-in with the imps was any indication, people were going to start turning up dead sooner rather than later.

You think they're packing up business? Maggie cut into my thoughts.

Maybe, I replied. *They abandoned the warehouse with three months' worth of rent already paid. People don't close up when business is good.*

So either business is bad, Maggie said thoughtfully.

Or, I replied, *they know that someone has caught on to their little scheme.*

I tried to work through a dozen different angles. It could be someone inside one of the soul collecting businesses, maybe a disgruntled or ex-employee. It could be an Other, like Maggie, who had limited omniscience and smelled trouble. It could even be a reaper gone bad. There were too damn many possibilities. I cursed Ferryman for bringing this to me instead of OtherOps and got back in my truck.

Where to? Maggie asked. *We're kind of out of leads.*

I looked at my hands on the steering wheel, running my eyes over my tattoos. The facsimile of Grendel's claw on the back of my left hand made the skin itch, dormant sorcery wanting to come to life. I considered going back to visit Zeke. I owed him a slap for siccing that necromancer on me, and he might be able to nudge me in a new direction. *There's still one good option,* I told Maggie.

What are you thinking... Oh, no. I don't think that's a good idea.

I started the car. *I don't either. But I've got a job to do, and Kappie Shuteye is the only one who might know what a bunch of imps are doing working for a soul thief.*

Alek...

I cut her off. *It's my next move. If you don't like it, go read a book.*

The words came out a little harsher than I intended, but I still remembered her anger at the necromancer. I get bossed around so much by Ada that I really didn't need it coming from Maggie too. This job was starting to give me tension headaches—not to mention that fact that it had already forced me to kill five people. I needed to move quickly and decisively.

Still, I wasn't above admitting—to myself—that Maggie might be right. After all, Kappie Shuteye is the imp king who sold me to Ada twenty years ago.

The term *imp king* sounds more impressive than it actually is. It would be more accurate to say something like *imp mob boss*, and for some of the people who've inherited the term, even that might be generous. All imp kings operate a little differently, but most of them amount to little more than a union overseer for their kind in a certain region. Their underlings bow and scape and pay their membership dues, and in return the imp king finds them steady work in his own ventures or hires them out to whoever is willing to pay for a little sleazy muscle.

Kappie Shuteye is imp king of northeast Ohio, but that hasn't always been his job. Back in the '70s and '80s, he sat on the board of directors of a company called Paronskaft. Their specialty was buying firstborn children in return for magical favors. In the reaper business, we call the children *rumpelstiltskins*, or *skins* for short. Paronskaft basically ran a slave trade until they were shut down in the late '80s. As far as I know, I was one of the last children sold by Paronskaft before OtherOps shuttered them for good. Kappie was the one who arranged the deal.

The last time I saw him, I broke his nose.

I pulled off the highway at a place called Brecksville, and pretty soon I turned into the parking lot of an old, run-down elementary school in an overgrown part of town that had once been a community of trailer parks. It looked like the school had been crumbling for decades: most of the windows were broken, the brick facade was barely in one piece, and the parking lot itself could barely be called concrete anymore. Despite the empty look of the place, there were at least a dozen cars parked in the teacher's lot around back, including a couple of flatbeds and an entire semitrailer. A team of imps loaded the semi with plastic-wrapped pallets of indeterminate origin. They all stopped to stare as I pulled up and parked.

I got out and leaned against the hood of my truck, letting the imps size me up for a moment. I took out my phone, pretended to scroll through it, and snapped a photo of the group, which I emailed to Nadine—a little insurance policy in case Kappie decided he wanted to rough me up for breaking his nose. "I'm looking for Kappie," I finally called to them.

None of them moved.

"I'll go find him myself if you want a stranger poking around," I said. One of the imps drew a knife. He and three of his friends took a step toward me. I did a quick count of the cars in the parking lot and decided that if fifty imps came pouring out of the old school, I'd probably be in for a rough time. I tried to act bored with their posturing and held up one hand. "Tell your boss that Alek Fitz from Valkyrie Collections is here to see him. I'm a reaper, so put your goddamn knife away."

Two of the imps broke off from the group and ran into

the bowels of the old school while their aggressive friend put his knife away without an apology. He gestured dismissively toward me. "Go in that door there. Wait just inside."

The door led to an old furnace room, which was recessed into the ground about two stories below me. There was a small, ground-level space just inside the door, and then a handful of catwalks that led above the boilers to the halls of the old school. I did a cursory look around, checking to see what had changed in the five years since I was last here—and if Kappie's imps had rigged any improvised traps. Imps love making things that can hurt people accidentally.

What do you think they're loading in that truck out there? Maggie asked me.

Drugs, probably. Can't you sense them?

Nah. There are low-level wards all over this place to protect against scrying. I'd have to be there in person to see through them. Why doesn't the city shut Kappie down? This whole setup is beyond obvious.

I'd guess that Kappie makes sizable donations to the mayor's office and local police force. Ambition isn't a common trait among imps. Ninety-nine point nine percent of them are vicious little creatures driven by greed and hunger, and they seldom have the ability to plan beyond the next fix, robbery, or minimum-wage paycheck. Imp kings are the remaining few who *do* have the ability to plan beyond those things.

The door at the other end of the catwalk suddenly opened, and a wizened old imp appeared. He was taller than most of his kind—probably five foot two—and wore a bright red zoot suit, matching hat, and wingtip shoes. The clothes, together with an imp's stereotypically squat, ugly face, made him look like a Dick Tracy villain. I would have laughed at his appearance if I didn't know that he liked to trick out that suit with a straight razor in one sleeve and a switchblade in the other.

"Alek Fitz!" he proclaimed in a gravelly voice, a salesman's smile on his face. "My old friend! How long has it been?"

"We're not friends, Kappie. The last time we saw each other, you took a swing at me with a straight razor and I broke your nose. How is that, by the way?"

"My face hurts every time it's cold."

I grinned at him. "It gets cold a lot in Cleveland."

Kappie's smile faltered. He took a step onto the catwalk, his head nodding slowly. "How is your lovely boss, Ada? She still working you to the bone?"

Keep cool, Maggie warned me.

"You know, I really wouldn't mind breaking your nose again."

"And I wouldn't mind burying your body on the premises, but I don't think you came here for either of those activities. How may I help you, Reaper Fitz?"

I rolled my eyes. "Got some questions for you, Kappie."

Kappie licked his lips like a fat man eyeing a succulent desert. "Questions? Questions? Have you joined OtherOps now, Alek? If that's the case, you should identify yourself immediately. Unless they've changed their handbook."

"I'm not with OtherOps." I resisted the urge to look around for a sink. Talking with imps always made me want to wash my hands, and Kappie was worse than most.

"Reapers aren't in the business of asking questions," Kappie rasped thoughtfully. "Unless you're here to ask my help in finding a debtor. In which case, we need to talk about a fee first."

"I'm curious if you know anything about a group of imps that wound up dead downtown yesterday."

Where are you taking this, Alek? Maggie asked. *Do you really want to tell him you killed five of his kind? He won't let you walk out of here alive.*

He's not going to find out who did it, I assured her.

Kappie raised thick eyebrows. "Dead imps? I haven't heard a word. Should I be expecting a visit from OtherOps?"

He's telling the truth, Maggie interjected.

"I doubt it," I said. "OtherOps doesn't know they're dead."

"Did you kill them?"

The question shouldn't have surprised me, but it did. I kept my expression neutral. "What business would I have killing imps?"

Kappie lifted his chin, eyeballing me down the bridge of his nose. "Because you hate us. Or you think imps are stealing from one of your clients."

"Are they?" I asked.

Kappie cocked an eyebrow, then leaned against the railing of the catwalk. "From your demeanor, I can assume that *someone* is. It's the only reason you would come out here. Beyond breaking my nose, that is. If you told me the name of the client who was robbed, I might be able to help..."

"Just answer the question: Have you or your kin been stealing from a Valkyrie client?"

"Not to my knowledge."

He's telling the truth, Maggie broke in again.

You're sure? There was definitely a part of me that had hoped Kappie would be involved in this mess so I had an excuse to bring Ferryman's wrath down on his head.

Sure as I can spot a liar.

"If you're lying to me," I told Kappie, "I'll rip your ears off."

Kappie seemed unaffected by the threat. "Now, now, Alek, no need for that kind of language. I'm not stupid. If you're out here asking questions, that means that OtherOps hasn't been involved yet. But if you fail, they *will* get involved, and dead imps will mean that they'll question me first. I'm the last person who wants that. I'm being entirely honest. Let me see here..." he tapped his chin. "Have you checked with my competitors?"

"You don't have competitors," I said cautiously.

"On the contrary—two of my former colleagues from Paronskaft have been pressing in on my territory lately.

This region has proven very profitable for some of my side businesses, and I won't let them have a cut."

"Do you have names?" I asked.

"Leave me a card, and I'll have one of my people send them over," Kappie said. I gave him my card, and he pocketed it. He paused, then added, "Call any of your contacts over at OtherOps. There's an imp turf war brewing in the Midwest. I've been trying to stay out of it, but my territory is at the heart of it. If some dead imps turned up, you can likely look toward one of the names I'll send you later."

I tapped my foot. I hadn't *entirely* convinced myself that Kappie was involved, but I definitely hadn't expected him to be so cooperative. "All right, send me those names. If you hear anything at all about stolen Other goods, let me know immediately." I turned and left before I had to look at his stupid face for any longer. I headed back to my truck, where I spent a few minutes watching imps load their semi while I meditated on his answer.

So everything he said is true? I asked Maggie again.

Or at least he believes it's true, she answered. *He's not responsible for Ferryman's missing souls. Could it be one of his competitors?*

Possibly, I said, *but I'm not going to rule him out just yet. He was too straightforward. I've never met an imp that willing to answer questions.*

Maybe he's scared of the people moving in on his territory, Maggie suggested. *If there's a bigger, badder imp out there gunning for his turf, it might be in his interest to be honest with us.*

An imp war. That's the last damn thing we need right now. I started the truck, then opened the glove compartment, sorted through a handful of loose cigars—an old tip from Baron Samedi—and pulled out a bag of honey-roasted cashews. Snacking away, I drove out of the parking lot and headed toward the highway. "You Spin Me Right Round" came on the radio. I hummed along, thinking aloud at Maggie. *I have my doubts that even an imp king is greedy enough to steal souls. Imps are involved—we've got a pile of their dead kin to prove it—but I have the feeling it's going to lead back to something more dangerous than these little assholes.*

What next? Maggie asked.

In answer, I dialed up Justin and listened to the ringer until his voice came on.

"Justin, it's Alek. Quick question for you."

"Hey! I was just about to call you. What's up?"

I drove with my knee, cashews in one hand, phone in the other. "Have you heard any whispers about an imp war?"

"Seriously?" He laughed. "There've been whispers about an imp war for years. When they start turning up dead in large numbers, I'll believe that one of those lazy asshole kings has finally decided to start something serious."

I sucked the salty-sweet flavor off one of the cashews, deep in thought. This didn't necessarily rule out the possibility that a war was coming, or that Kappie was afraid of one. But if Justin didn't find the idea credible, I leaned toward believing him. "So," I asked slowly, "if I were to send you some pictures of some imps, could you run IDs on them with no questions asked?"

"Sure."

"I'm serious. *No questions.*"

"Eh, nobody around here cares much for imps, and we still owe you for that thing with the bunyip. Yeah, I can do that."

"Thanks. I'll buy the first two rounds next time we're out. Oh, what were you about to call me about?"

"That necromancer kid."

"He give you anything?"

"No, but our examiner finished with him. That kid is stupid powerful. We actually had to overnight special restraints for him so he wouldn't have to be under personal guard twenty-four seven. I'm not sure if that actually matters or not, but I thought you'd want to know. If you hadn't broken his fingers, he probably would've killed you in that Starbucks."

I growled in frustration. I still needed to know who hired him. "Thanks for the info. I'll send you photos of imps to ID." I hung up and tapped the corner of the phone against my bottom canines to the tune of whatever was on the radio as I sought after one of those many niggling thoughts that had crept past me while talking to Kappie. I dialed Nadine.

When she picked up, I said, "Nadine, I need you to do a little hunting for me."

"What kind of hunting, hun?"

"Something's been bothering me about that thing with Judith Pyke. First, who would know that she lost her soul, and second, who would be in a position to know that she was disgruntled over the whole thing?"

"Is that a question?"

"No, I'm thinking out loud. Do this for me: call LuciCorp and see if you can get anything else out of her file—whether someone who works there happens to be friends with her, or if her old case worker might have gotten a windfall recently."

"That's a lot of ground to cover."

"I appreciate the help." I hung up before she could protest further. I'd need to call Judith and ask her a few more questions, but that could wait until I had some more coffee in me. I was in a relatively rural area, and I despaired of having to wait until I was back to the freeway to find a Starbucks. Pulling up to a stop sign, I put away my cashews so I wouldn't eat the whole bag in one sitting. When I sat back up, I saw a brief flash of metal out of the corner of my eye and heard Maggie scream in my ear.

Look out!

The world exploded in glass and twisting steel.

CHAPTER 7

Wake up. Wake up! WAKE UP!

Pain shot through me, lancing upward from my left hand and spreading through my body like a fire. For a few moments, I thought my finger had been cut off. I jerked my head up and away from the wall of the truck's cab, trying to blink through a haze of double vision. A black car had jumped the ditch and slammed into the passenger-side wheel well of my truck. A mix of smoke and steam rose from the engines of both vehicles. I shook my hand violently and held it to my face until I realized that the pain was coming from Maggie's ring and not a wound.

I'm awake! I told her. *What happened?*

Two draugr are getting out of that car. They will be at your door in less than ten seconds, and they have every intention of killing you.

How long have I been out?

Moments, she answered. *Get the fuck out of your truck.*

I felt like I was moving through molasses as I tried to open the door. The whole frame of the truck had been twisted by the accident, and I had to put my shoulder against the door and give it a hard shove before it creaked open. Too much strength went into the shove, and I tottered out of the vehicle, my legs wobbly beneath me, and I slipped on the steep, muddy bank of the ditch my truck had been pushed into. I fell to my hands and knees and squeezed my eyes shut for a brief moment.

Move it, damn you. On your feet!

Maggie's urging got me to my knees, then my feet. I could feel my muscles in that post-car-accident disjointedness, when the stiffness hasn't set in yet but your body knows something is wrong. My vision finally began to clear as the two draugr came around the front of my ruined truck. They looked, somehow, more... full than last time—meatier, taller, though their eyes were still hollow. One of them stopped, leaning over the bumper like it was looking for something, while the other came straight toward me at a run.

It leapt at me like a lion, arms out, razor-like fingernails hitting me full in the chest. I felt them bite into my tough skin as I grabbed him by the forearms and spun, using his momentum to throw him over my shoulder. The toss was successful, but I slipped on the muddy ditch again and went down into shin-deep, stagnant water. I splashed across and climbed the other side after my opponent.

The draugr was back on its feet by the time I reached it. I eyed its stance as it prepared to throw itself at me again, seeing absolutely no amount of finesse in the movement. Whoever this asshole had been in real life, it had not been a fighter.

Which didn't mean it wasn't insanely strong.

Mjolnir flared to life on the back of my hand. My knuckles connected with its chest, but unlike last time, my fist didn't breeze through it like paper. Its sorcery-infused body buckled under the blow, bones grinding beneath the power of my tattoo but not giving way entirely. The draugr snatched at my elbow with its one good hand, its nails drawing blood, and tried to bury its blacked teeth in my neck.

The "remove its spine and watch it disappear" trick wasn't going to work again. These guys had clearly gotten a makeover not just for their physical forms but for the sorcery holding them together. I got my left arm between my neck and the draugr's gnashing teeth and backpedaled under the force of the draugr's momentum. That force suddenly disappeared, and the draugr stepped back so abruptly that I nearly tripped backward over my own feet. I had just enough time for a moment of confusion before I remembered the other draugr.

I whirled and caught a glimpse of the chrome bumper of

my truck swinging toward me like a baseball bat. The bumper caught me just beneath the chin, snapping my mouth closed, my head back, and my whole body into an unplanned backflip.

Pain lanced through me like electricity as I landed in the grass. It came from both my ringing head and my finger.

Don't you dare pass out! Maggie shouted.

I propped myself up on my forearms. *If I get hold of this bastard again, flame him.*

No can do. We have company.

I didn't have time to figure out what she meant. I heard footsteps coming fast, and I rolled on pure instinct. The end of the bumper slammed into the grass where I'd just been. I tried to get to my knees only for the next swing to tag me on the shoulder. I flipped around and finally rolled to my knees just as another swing came for my head.

I caught the bumper with both hands. My tusks were completely out now, blood streaming from my torn gums and bashed-up chin. Red mist clouded my vision. "That's mine," I said, wrenching the bumper out of the second draugr's grip. In such close quarters it wasn't going to do me much good, so I discarded it and came up swinging with my left hand.

My Mjolnir tattoo might not have punched through the brute-force sorcery animating a draugr, but Grendel's claw didn't need to. I brought my hand up vertically and perfectly flat, like an upward karate chop, and caught draugr right in the center of the sternum. The tips of my fingers sliced through bone and tissue like a knife blade, bisecting its sternum, punching through the top of its spine, and then slicing its entire skull perfectly in half.

The draugr disappeared in a scattering of dust.

I stumbled through the cloud, coughing in the remains, and managed to take a second to get my bearings. I looked up to find that a pair of pickups had pulled up to the crash while we'd fought. Imps had piled out of them and now stood at a safe distance to watch. Among them was Kappie

Shuteye, grinning from ear to ear at my blood-covered face.

The other draugr was limping toward our crashed cars and holding its shoulder. My Mjolnir tattoo must have done more damage than I'd thought. The fiend glanced over its shoulder as it crossed the ditch and, though it had no eyes, its body language betrayed a wariness that hadn't been there before.

I wasn't sure if the draugr had some kind of weapon in the car it meant to retrieve or if it planned on escaping to fight again another day. I had no intention of letting it do either. I snatched up my bumper and sprinted after the draugr. I jumped the ditch just as it reached the driver's side of its car. Swinging the bumper up and over my shoulder, I brought it down in the middle of the draugr's skull.

I was, to be honest, more than a little shocked when he didn't disintegrate immediately with such a powerful blow. His skull bounced off the hood of his car and twisted around, hanging on to the spine by a few willowy sinews. Head on backward, the draugr hissed at me.

Mjolnir flared. I put my right fist through its teeth and watched it fade to dust.

I staggered forward, seeing double for a moment, and leaned on the hood of the car. It took a few moments to clear the blurriness from my vision, and when I did, I saw Kappie standing out at the front of his imps, chuckling happily to himself.

"We heard the car crash and came to see what happened," Kappie said.

I pointed at the car. "You have anything to do with this?"

"That? Not me," he said. He was so pleased with himself that I wanted to put my fist through *his* teeth. In fact, I was struggling not to. This close on the heels of a fight, the haze of troll berserker was still trying to gain control of my mind. All the hate and revulsion I felt for Kappie wasn't helping things. My hands balled instinctually into fists, my tusks aching as I tried to get them to retract.

You all right, big guy? Maggie asked cautiously.

I fought with my base, violent instincts. *Is he lying?* I finally asked.

No. All truth. He had nothing to do with this.

Kappie walked over to me slowly, twirling his cane, and gave the crash site—and then the grass where I'd fought the two draugr—a considering glance. His eyes settled on my tusks. "How powerful of a necromancer did you piss off?" he asked.

I blinked a couple more times. The berserker haze finally began to clear. "What are you talking about?"

He tapped his cane on the thin layer of dust on the concrete. "Draugr will rise multiple times if the summoner is powerful enough, and those guys looked like they'd already been killed once."

"I have no idea what you're talking about." I really didn't. I was finding it hard to think through the stiffness, the bleeding, and the sudden onset of a screaming headache.

Kappie continued to grin. "If reanimated by a strong enough necromancer," he said slowly, as if explaining to a thick child, "draugr can't be killed. Destroy them, and they'll reform in their graves. You have to put them down for good." He pointed his cane emphatically at my chest.

I pushed it aside and staggered to my car, where I searched among the broken glass for my phone. It was, thankfully, undamaged. *Is he right about the draugr thing?* I asked Maggie.

Uh, yeah. Yeah, he is. She sounded awfully sheepish.

I narrowed my eyes. *You knew about this?*

I didn't think he was that powerful! she protested.

I sighed and dialed 911. "I'm calling the cops," I told Kappie. "Unless you guys are gonna give witness statements…" The imps were all back in their cars by the time someone answered the phone. I took a step back, reported the crime, and then stood there, staring at my twisted wreck of a truck while I waited for the cops to arrive.

Chapter 8

I got a call from Nadine the next afternoon while I sat at a Cracker Barrel, having a late lunch. "Alek," I answered.

"How are you feeling today, hun?" Nadine asked.

"Like I got hit by a car, funny enough," I answered flatly. My troll blood let me shrug off a lot of damage, but everything ached badly, and that headache was still floating around the back of my skull. I wanted nothing more than to lie down and sleep it off for a few days, but that wasn't going to happen.

"You should go to the doctor. Get some oxy."

"I don't have time for that shit." I'd taken a triple dose of aspirin, and it would have to be enough. I couldn't afford to be foggy-headed this week.

"I can get you a little weed if you need it."

"It's never done jack for me."

"Sorry, hun. Let me know if there's anything I can do."

"I appreciate it, Nadine. What's up?"

I heard her tapping something out on her keyboard. "Have you checked your email today?" she asked.

"Not for a few hours. I've been hitting up a few more informants to try to dig up more leads."

"Anything?"

"Nope."

"Well, you'll get there. Your buddy over at OtherOps has sent you an ID on one of those dead imps. He cc'd me on the email to make sure you got it."

I took the phone away from my ear long enough to check. "Yup, it's there. I appreciate it. Did LuciCorp give you any more information on Judith?"

"They just sent over her file. I'm going to comb through it today and tomorrow."

"Thanks." I hung up and opened the email from Justin. All it said was *heads up*, but it had two PDF attachments. They turned out to be a pair of dossiers. The first was of the dead imp—his name, known associates, known addresses, and a list of misdemeanors he'd been attached to over the last fifteen years. The second dossier was far more interesting because it belonged to the dead imp's brother, who was, according to OtherOps' information, still alive and well and living in a group home for imps out in Ashtabula County.

Ugh, Maggie said as I paid my bill and headed out to my rented Prius. *I hate Ashtabula—trailer parks and meth houses as far as the eye can see.*

I like it, I told her. *The old reapers used to take me out to a little fair there every so often when I went on ride-alongs as a kid. I wonder if that place is still around. I loved the bumper cars.*

Ashtabula is the armpit of Ohio, Maggie insisted.

I grinned. *Ohio has a lot of armpits, and we love them all.*

I hopped on the freeway and drove east, soon lost in my own thoughts as I tried to unravel this thing Ferryman had brought me into. Imps tend to work in family units, so the dead imp's brother seemed like a pretty good shot at picking up a lead. Even if he wasn't directly involved in what his brother was doing, he'd definitely have some idea what it was. If I couldn't make him talk, I'd drag him back to Kappie, who would be far more interested in throwing one of his underlings to the wolves than getting involved with my clients.

I still couldn't fathom what kind of creature would think it wise to steal from the Lords of Hell. The human who rented the warehouse in the flats might be my best bet. Humans were always more unpredictable than any of the Other, and I could think of few Other with the guts or stupidity to try and cheat Death. Those that were... well, most of them were gods, or beings *way* above my pay grade. Assuming it *was* a human, how rich or powerful did they have to be to hire imps out from underneath the nose of the local imp king? Maybe, I decided, this culprit was a half-breed like me.

I pulled myself out of my thoughts as my GPS led me down a long, single-lane drive in a town called North Kingsville. It was about an hour since I'd received the call from Nadine. I came to a stop thirty yards from an old beat-up plastic mailbox marked with the address I'd been given and looked across the overgrown lawn to a run-down bungalow with ancient, post–World War II wooden siding and a moss-covered roof. A thick forest surrounded the yard, and opposite the house was an overgrown farmer's field.

I felt Maggie's presence in the ring—a slight warmth that indicated she was alert and examining our surroundings with apt attention. Strangely, she did not comment as I got out of the car and stood next to it. I watched for any sign of movement. The front door of the house was open, and there were five rusted old cars and trucks parked in the grass in front. I couldn't hear any noise or see any sign of life. I didn't need Maggie to tell me something was wrong.

I got my shoulder holster and Glock out of my endless wallet and put them on before walking slowly toward the mailbox.

Despite the disrepair of the place, there were many signs of occupancy. Besides the cars by the drive, grass was trampled by tire tracks all along the drive and yard, as if they'd recently thrown a big house party here. I smelled smoke and soon caught sight of the smoldering remains of a bonfire around the other side of the house.

It didn't take long to catch the smell of ammonia on the breeze. I took a handkerchief out of my endless wallet and tied it around my face. *Meth house,* I told Maggie. *It's probably one of Kappie's. He owns dozens around Cleveland.*

There's nothing alive inside that house. It wasn't just the words Maggie used that brought me to a standstill, but the tone in which she said them. They were whispered angrily, with a slight hiss like a cornered cat. My tusks began to emerge on their own, and I had to force them back down, painfully, through my tender gums.

What do you mean? I asked her.

I mean that house if full of corpses, Maggie replied. *Something isn't right here. You should go. Now.*

I raised my eyebrows. I was a little beat up from yesterday, but Maggie knew better than anyone that I could take care of myself in a scrap. My heart began to hammer. *Is there danger?* I asked.

Yes.

What is it?

I don't know. You should go.

Despite Maggie's warnings, I inched closer. There could be answers in this house—answers worth a little risk. Heart hammering, I drew my Glock, holding it at the ready, and rounded the mailbox. Maggie remained silent. I could feel her uncertainty like a weight in the pit of my stomach. I crossed the caved-in porch carefully and looked through the doorway.

The door wasn't just open; it had been ripped from its hinges and lay inside the dimly lit front room. Ammonia made my eyes water as I squinted at the inside and caught my first whiff of death. With a deep breath, I hopped a broken porch plank and stepped inside. Something squelched beneath my boots, and it took me a few moments to realize that the ratty old carpet was literally soaked with blood. I froze in my tracks and took in the scene.

The living room was covered in the pieces of what had once been six or seven imps. A head sat in the center of the room as if carefully placed there to watch for intruders. It was surrounded by arms, legs, and bits of flesh and innards literally strewn about the place like confetti. The blood spatter across the walls was so thick that at first I thought it had been painted on. I gagged, swallowed bile, and forced myself across the squishing carpet.

The kitchen had another two dead imps inside. These appeared more or less intact. One had been disemboweled from behind as he'd tried to flee toward the back door, and the other had his throat torn out. He still held an unfired shotgun in his stiff hands. Broken glass, metal plates, and single-burner cooktops covered the entire kitchen—the shattered remnants of a rather extensive meth lab. The back door was also open, its ripped screen door creaking in the breeze.

Look down. Maggie told me.

I looked at my feet to see a single enormous footprint. It was at least eighteen inches long and six inches wide. One big pad and three little ones, along with four toes and the scratches of big talons, were distinctly outlined by the blood. The footprint was clearly pointed toward the door, as if whatever made it had killed these last two imps as an afterthought as it leapt into the night.

Werewolf? Maggie asked.

Possibly, I told her, sniffing for the telltale scent of wet dog. I couldn't get anything over the ammonia burn in my nostrils. I went back into the other room and checked a torso. Bite marks covered the shoulder and stomach. Whatever had been here very clearly gnawed on the poor bastards. *No self-respecting werewolf I know about would eat imp meat, not even in a fury. It would have to be starving. Maybe a wendigo?*

They usually don't come this far south. And they wouldn't eat imp, either. Not when there's plenty of isolated houses around here where they could grab a fresh human.

I did a quick circuit of the house, using my phone to take pictures of the carnage in the living room and kitchen and three more bodies I found in the back bedroom. I stepped outside and allowed myself a moment to dry heave into the bushes before dialing a number.

"Yeah?" a voice answered.

"Justin," I said. "That address you sent me this morning? I just got here. Something very big and angry got here before me and killed everyone in the house. Send a team out here right away. And no, I'm not going to wait. I'm getting the hell out of here before whatever it is decides to come back for a snack." I hung up and went around the side of the house.

You're definitely getting out of here, right? Maggie asked.

In a moment, I said. I told myself that the dread in my stomach was just from seeing those corpses. There wasn't anything in these woods but me and the dead, and nobody would be here from OtherOps for at least forty minutes. I needed to look around. I walked the perimeter of the yard quickly, hoping to find more evidence of whatever had done this. Strangely, I found nothing—no more bloody prints, and not even any bent grass or broken branches from something large blundering into the underbrush.

I checked each of the cars. None seemed damaged or disturbed in any way. One still had the keys in the ignition and the driver's-side door open, as though an imp had stopped by to grab something from the house and been caught in the butchery.

I circled the house two more times before heading over to the remnants of the bonfire. It was a pile of ash perhaps seven feet across, with small refuse and twigs still half burned around the edges. The head of a child's doll lay nearby, with a matching foot among the remaining trash. I picked up a stick and poked around in the ash, wondering if this bonfire had happened before or after the deaths of the imps.

Alek.

What is it? I replied.

Time to go.

Is OtherOps here already? I tilted my head, listening for the sound of a car, and then realized Maggie was whispering again.

No. We're being watched.

The hair on the back of my neck stood on end. I casually got to my feet, Glock still gripped in one hand, and circled the bonfire while glancing cautiously toward the tree line. *Human? Maybe a neighbor?*

Definitely not. Whatever it is, my sorcery slides right past it.

I swallowed hard and resisted the urge to run toward my car. I may be a tough son of a bitch, but I had no interest in tangling with something that could mow through this many imps without, apparently, missing a beat. I took a deep breath. *Can you give me a location?*

No. Just leave. She sounded genuinely worried. She might be a powerful Other, but she was trapped on *my* finger, and I was mostly human.

I took a few steps toward the car when something caught my eye—a glint among the ashes of the bonfire. I knelt quickly, reaching into the warm ash, and plucked out a small mirror. I forgot my fear immediately and began sifting through the ash. Within moments I had three more mirrors in my hands.

I fled toward the car, and didn't even breathe until I was back on the interstate. The mirrors lay on the passenger seat. I couldn't stop glancing at them or my rearview mirror.

We aren't being followed, Maggie informed me.

Any idea what that was back there? I asked. A cold sweat trickled down the small of my back.

The killer, or whatever, was watching us?

Either. Both.

No on both accounts.

Maggie is very good at knowing things. It's what jinn do. The fact that she couldn't pinpoint the creature we were dealing with made me more nervous than the bodies.

Are those mirrors what I think they are? she asked.

Soul mirrors, I confirmed. *Those imps were definitely working the same job as the ones we killed downtown.*

They're working for someone else right under Kappie's nose.

I lifted one of the mirrors, taking my eyes off the road long enough to get a good, long look at it. Unless I was mistaken, this mirror had an occupant: one of Ferryman's missing souls. And I was willing to bet that whoever was employing the imps also had them killed to cover his tracks.

Chapter 9

I sat in my office in the Valkyrie building later that night, long after everyone else had gone home. I leaned back in my chair, feet on my desk, flipping though the soul mirrors that I'd recovered from that bonfire. To the casual observer—even to someone who knew a lot about the Other—these were just a couple of handheld mirrors. They could have come from a car or a discarded child's play set or a makeup box. I doubted that half the people at OtherOps would have given them a second glance. Whoever had thrown them in that fire had known enough to want to destroy them but had *not* known that soul mirrors are next to impossible to break. A bonfire certainly wouldn't crack them.

I set the mirrors on my desk and picked up my phone, scanning through the hundreds of pictures I'd taken over the last few days. Most of them were different angles of dead imps. I moved through them quickly until I got to a number of pictures I'd taken of Judith Pyke. I zoomed in on her emaciated face and thought over our conversation. Hopefully she'd already left town, ahead of whoever or whatever was trying to clean up loose ends. After a few moments, I exited out of the pictures and searched through my wallet until I found Ferryman's business card.

I turned it over, looking at the mirror on the back, and then set the card facedown on the table in front of me. I pressed three fingers against the glass.

The world crinkled around me, and I immediately found myself standing in murky darkness. I'd been through enough stepping mirrors that I didn't stumble upon arriving in this new place. I tried to get my bearings, failed, and cleared my throat.

A light winked into existence a few yards to my left. It

came from a bedside-style reading lamp clamped to a card table, at which Ferryman sat regarding a game of solitaire laid out in front of him. He clutched a cigarette between his fingers. Ferryman didn't seem to notice my presence, so I walked over to join him, my boots echoing like I was walking across a blackened gymnasium at night.

"Is this your place?" I asked. My voice whispered back at me, more like a mocking mimic than an echo.

"It is," Ferryman answered.

"Is it really a good idea to hand out business cards that have a stepping mirror directly to Death's realm?"

Ferryman put a jack on a queen and leaned back, giving me a distracted look. "You don't think I can control who uses my stepping mirror?"

"Fair point." I rounded the table to stand in front of Ferryman, briefly wondering what Death's realm would look like if I shone a flashlight through the darkness. It was probably filled with skulls or spirits or something equally macabre—either that, or endless nothing. I thought of the description he'd given of himself doing paperwork for the dead. Maybe filing cabinets? I wasn't sure which would be worse.

You there? I nudged Maggie.

No, she said. *I'm hiding.*

Come on. You're being a huge scaredy cat lately.

That's because we're getting mixed up in things out of our league. You can wander into Death's realm if you'd like, but you should have left me at the office.

Yes, because I can just slip your ring off whenever I want, remember?

"I assume you're here because you have a status update?" Ferryman asked. "Your clients are getting antsy about this whole thing, you know."

I snorted at both him and Maggie. "It's been what, five days? And I'm pretty sure *you're* my client. The fact that you're a middleman for the Lords of Hell has little to do with our business arrangement."

"Me, them—it doesn't matter all that much, does it?" Ferryman gave me a sallow smile.

"If you're so worried, you should have come forward earlier."

Would you please stop being sassy with Death? Maggie grumbled.

"I didn't know about it earlier," Ferryman claimed.

I thought about Judith Pyke. "I'm pretty sure you're lying."

Jesus Christ, Alek!

Ferryman finally turned his attention entirely away from his card game and scowled at me. "Now, why would that be in my best interest?"

"Because there's something going on that you'd rather not tell me, even in confidence. But I'm neck-deep in your investigation. Time to fess up." Ferryman glared hard at me, unresponsive. Once the silence had gone on long enough to be awkward, I removed the soul mirrors from my pocket and tossed them on the card table. "Do these have souls in them?"

Ferryman inhaled sharply. He picked up one of the mirrors and held it under his reading light. He checked the next mirror, then the next. "Five of the missing souls," he proclaimed, setting them to one side. "I am pleased."

"If you're pleased, tell me what's going on."

Ferryman's eyes narrowed.

"I did the math," I continued. "That soul on top of the stack? I pulled that out of a woman named Judith Pyke. It had been sold to her secondhand by a group of imps. Having it in her body was killing her—fast. As far as I can tell, the imps planned on taking the soul back from her when she was too weak to fight them. They kill her, sell the soul to another poor sap, and the cycle continues. A way to make money in the mortal realm with otherwise useless souls, right?"

Ferryman nodded unhappily.

I went on. "Now, you told me that when a person dies,

their soul returns to your realm to be reunited with their shade and become a full spirit again. You also mentioned that physical possession of the soul upon the death of the body is important. What I want to know is what happens when someone other than the Lords of Hell is in possession of the soul upon the original vessel's death. And why is it such a big deal to you, personally?"

Ferryman let out a long-suffering sigh. I doubted anyone had ever questioned him this closely about how all this stuff worked. To most mortals, it was beyond their care or comprehension. To the Other, it was just business as usual. He dragged his arm across the table, erasing the game of solitaire and gathering the cards into a stack. He shuffled them twice and set the stack to one side. "Ada did warn me that you were persistent."

"I'm just doing my job," I said with a spike of annoyance. "And it's easier to do when clients are honest with me."

He leaned back in his rickety folding chair and took a drag on his cigarette. "It's all about contracts. The Lords of Hell, the Avatars of Heaven, and hundreds of other organizations contract with *me* to store the shades, reunite them with souls, and send the spirits on to wherever they're meant to go. If a person dies and is still in possession of their soul, it naturally seeks out the shade to be reunited. I don't actually have to do anything in that case. If they are *not* in possession of their soul, then the soul must be brought to me by whoever has it."

"So stolen souls means that you've got shades that can't be reunited with their other half?"

"Exactly."

I tried to ignore the goose bumps on the backs of my hands. "What happens if a soul and a shade are not reconnected?"

"It's annoying, but I deal with it. The soul will always end up here eventually." Ferryman grunted. "*That's* not the problem."

"Then what is?"

Ferryman took another long drag on his cigarette. I could practically see him deciding how much to tell me. "The problem," he finally said, "is that shades are dying."

I frowned. "I'm guessing that's not normal?"

"It's not. Just like souls and spirits, shades are forever. Immutable. My realm is made up of billions of shades, all waiting to be reunited with their souls."

"And when a shade dies?"

"It sends my realm into chaos."

Something in Ferryman's voice set off alarm bells in my head. I wasn't the only one. I could sense Maggie's presence listening carefully from within the ring. "What do you mean?"

"Imagine..." Ferryman picked up a single playing card and tapped it against his chin. "Imagine that you own a home, and the ground shifts very slightly beneath it. Not a proper earthquake, but a definite shift. Cracks appear in the drywall. Pipes come out of alignment. Now imagine that as the shifting intensifies, so does the damage. As the keeper of this place, I'm tasked with maintenance."

"You're running around with a can of stucco trying to keep things looking nice?"

"Something like that." Ferryman gave me his wan smile again. "Now imagine that your house has a mind of its own, and when the maintenance isn't properly kept up, it likes to lash out against the mortal realm." He began to lay out a new game of solitaire. "The last time my realm became unbalanced was when it was affected by a war between minor gods back in the fourteenth century. It lashed out in pain. Humanity got the Black Plague."

My eyes widened. "Didn't that kill two hundred million people?"

"One hundred seventy-three million, eight hundred forty-two thousand, six hundred and one, to be exact."

That number was way too specific for my liking. My goose

bumps intensified. "You're saying that if shades keep dying, your realm is gonna murder humanity?"

"Oh, it won't be anything that large. It's more likely to be an earthquake or a flu epidemic or something relatively minor. But it'll still hurt. A lot of people will die."

I ran through my hair. "That's a damn lot of pressure you've put me under."

"There's a reason I didn't tell you this in the first place."

"Thanks," I said, not bothering to hide my sarcasm. I began to pace. "Okay, so what's killing the shades?"

"All of those two hundred seventeen missing souls should have been processed into my realm over the new year."

"You mean that all the original owners died?"

"Yes. It's *their* shades that are dying."

A light went on in the back of my head. "It's because they're putting the used souls into other people's bodies?"

"I couldn't figure it out myself until you brought me the information on Judith Pyke, but I suspect that is the case."

"And what do we do about it?"

He cocked an eyebrow. "You're doing it."

I threw my hands in the air. "You're Death! Can't you just deal with this?"

"You of all people should know how important the Rules are. This is as involved as I can get in the mortal realm."

"Then you should have handed it straight to OtherOps. The actual cops should be doing this this, not me."

Ferryman snorted. "OtherOps might get results, yes, but they're a bureaucracy. Those results will come in six months, or maybe a year. That's not quick enough. And even if I convince OtherOps of the severity of the situation and they move lightning fast, they *will* let it slip to the public. It'll cause mass panics, suicides, and humans and Other turning against each other. The Lords of Hell will see their business dry up overnight."

"This is corporate protectionism?"

Ferryman stared at his newly laid out game. "I suppose it is."

"You're a prick." For once, Maggie didn't scold me. She floated on the edge of my awareness, still quiet, still listening.

"I've been called worse," Ferryman said as he leaned over his game and began to move cards. "I *do* think I have time, though I'm not sure how much. A couple of weeks? A month? I'm giving you ten more days before I pull the contract and alert OtherOps." He looked up, fixing me with those black, galaxy-speckled eyes. "I do have faith in you, Alek. Otherwise, I wouldn't have bothered. OtherOps may have resources, but you know this world. You know the clients and their customers and the equipment being used. A reaper is a far better agent to deal with this than an entire OtherOps office."

"Kind of you to say," I responded wryly. If Ferryman pulled the contract, I would have failed to stop a disaster, *and* Ada would be pissed as hell over losing out on however much Ferryman had offered her. Millions, no doubt. The two different sets of stakes seemed immeasurably imbalanced. But one would happen to the other people. The other would happen to *me*.

I took a few calming breaths and tried to pull myself together. Nothing to do now but go through with my investigation. I pointed at the mirrors on Ferryman's table. "I'm on the right track."

"It seems you are. As I said before, I am very pleased. You mentioned imps. Do you think they're behind this secondhand soul business?"

"I know they're *involved*. I doubt they're *behind* it. Imps are rarely behind anything but petty theft and drug dealing. I think they're working for someone both bolder and stupider." I paused, massaging the gums of my lower canines. "The truth is, I need the resources of someone like OtherOps. I haven't even explored *where* they're getting all these souls—

how they're stealing from reaper agencies or the Lords of Hell. Unfortunately, I have a thousand different angles to work, and it's just me."

"Keep on this trail of dead imps," Ferryman advised. "As I told you before, the Lords of Hell have conducted their own investigations and come up with nothing. Searching around in their trash cans isn't going to help."

That reminder tickled something in the back of my head. I couldn't quite put my finger on it. "That's... discouraging," I said. "It's possible that whoever is running this business has already figured out that we're on to them. He killed a whole bunch of his imps and tried to destroy some soul mirrors. If I had to guess, I'd say we have a few days at best before he finishes liquidizing his business and skips town."

"You'd better hurry, then."

"Thanks for the advice." I turned around, searching the darkness for the other side of the stepping mirror I'd come through, expecting a glint in the darkness. Nothing stood out. "I'll try to pick up the pace. In the meantime, make sure that Lucy and her friends answer their damn phones the moment I call."

"That won't be a problem," Ferryman promised.

"Good. Now, how the hell do I get back to my—" I hadn't finished my sentence when I found myself sitting back at my desk, my fingers still pressed to the stepping mirror. "Office." I blinked at the bright lighting and sighed, wishing I could go back and undo that whole conversation. My stomach was a knot now, a ball of stress that might just kill me before Death's realm could lash out at humanity like an angry child.

Answers aren't always fun, are they? Maggie asked.

No. Definitely not. The thought tickled the back of my brain again. There was something there, just outside of reach.

I do have some good news, Maggie told me. *I managed to find out how to put draugr to rest.*

At least that's something. How long until they show up and try to kill me again?

Based on the last time, you've got two more days. Maybe less. If we catch them while they regenerate, we might be able to get some information out of them.

I like the sound of that. Okay, tell me what we need, and we'll go have a talk with our undead friends.

Maggie hesitated. *My anniversary starts Friday afternoon.*

I know, I told her, feeling a flash of guilt. *That's why I want to get info out of them. If I can't spend your anniversary with you, at the very least I can give you a lead on who it is that knows you're still alive.*

Chapter 10

It was almost three in the morning when I pulled onto a quiet street just south of Mayfield Road on the eastern border of the Cleveland city limits. I sang along with Eurythmics' "Sweet Dreams (Are Made of This)" on the radio, squinting at signs until I found one advertising all-night parking. I got out, shrugging on an unlabeled hoodie and getting a Maglite from the passenger seat of my rental. I looked up and down the street, eyeballing the darkness for cops. The only sign of life I saw was a couple making out beneath a stop sign a block away.

The sight of them caused a stab of melancholy. It happened from time to time, especially when I was working late at night. I leaned on the car door, willing it away, trying not to think about the fact that my last girlfriend had dumped me after three weeks because I worked too much. That had been a couple years ago, and I'd had nothing but the occasional bar hookup since. As much as I liked Maggie, the fact that my only constant companion was a seven-century-old jinn was a tad dehumanizing.

The melancholy finally passed, and Maggie didn't seem to have noticed. *Hey, Mags, are we clear?* I could see my breath as a white fog beneath the flickering of the street light.

We're good, Maggie told me.

You're sure about that?

Yeah. Closest cop is half asleep, eating a donut three streets over from here.

Oh, come on, I told her. *That's racist.*

Cops aren't a race.

Coppist?

Is it coppist if he really is eating a donut? she asked.

I should ask Justin.

I checked my pocket for a pair of plastic baggies filled with some draugr dust I'd scraped up after our fight the other day. There was more dirt, gravel, and glass from my pickup windshield than there was actual draugr dust in either bag, but Maggie claimed it was enough. I flipped up my hood and walked quickly down the sidewalk, keeping an eye out for passing cars.

I crossed Mayfield Road and pulled myself over a seven-foot concrete wall, dropping on the other side to land in an overgrown tangle of vines, discarded stones, and the trees that formed a screen between the road and Lake View Cemetery. I knelt among the vines, squinting through the trees to the open grass and winding concrete paths that made up the cemetery beyond.

I spotted a flashlight bobbing in the darkness off to my left just as Maggie said, *Security,* and I moved behind a tree until he passed.

Rub a little more of that draugr dust on my ring, Maggie told me.

Kinky, I replied, following her instructions. I could practically feel her rolling her eyes.

Okay, I got it, she told me. *They're both in the same tomb. Head north until I say so.*

With Maggie guiding the way, I was able to navigate to the nearest path and follow in the security guard's footsteps. There was just enough moonlight that I could manage without my Maglite, but I kept it in hand regardless. We passed hundreds of graves varying as much in shape and size as the people within them. Black obelisks towered high above, and shadowy mausoleums seemed to menace me from the darkness. Despite working with loa, vampires, and even Death, cemeteries still gave me the willies.

How much do you think you'd have to be paid to be a security guard at a cemetery? I asked Maggie.

I'm a jinn. I'm not really scared of the dead.

Not even the undead?

Only ghouls. They're undead jinn.

Oh, that's a pleasant thought. I considered the small amount of Maggie's power she was able to use from within the ring and decided I didn't want to see that in the hands of a vengeful undead.

Mean bastards, Maggie said. *I've never had to tangle with one myself, but I've heard a pack of them can kill even the strongest ifrit.* Ifrit were a class of powerful infernal spirits—a type of jinn to which Maggie was closely related.

I was about to reply when I felt her ring nudge me down a side path toward the northeast corner of the cemetery. I dodged another security guard, and within minutes I was standing before a marble mausoleum about the size of a one-car garage. I checked over my shoulder, then risked my Maglite.

The mausoleum was tucked into a space off the beaten path and behind several large trees. It was overgrown with moss and ivy, the lettering above the iron-grate door so worn it was impossible to read. Upon closer inspection, I found the door wasn't locked or even closed all the way. A chain lay on the ground just inside the entrance, its links snapped rather than cut.

I took a hesitant step inside the mausoleum. There wasn't a lot of space—just two stone sarcophagi in a dark, damp interior. It looked like something out of a vampire film, except with way less space. An old-fashioned light bulb sconce hung from the center of the ceiling. I couldn't find a switch to turn it on, so I relied on my Maglite.

The sarcophagi had matching marble lids. One had the name TREVOR carved into the top, while the other said JACOB. They were born in 1798. One died 1874, the other 1877.

Twins, I'm guessing, I said to Maggie. *I wonder if that made it easier for the necromancer to raise them both.* I did a quick examination of the lids and found scratches where lid met base. *Definitely the right place.* I set my Maglite on one sarcophagus and emptied my pockets beside it: a bag of draugr dust, a wooden stake, a two-pound iron ingot, and a thin piece of sturdy cord. I eyed the assortment dubiously. *You sure this is going to work?*

Oh, not at all. It's not like I've tried all this shit out before—I found it in a book.

You're really doing great things for my confidence. I leaned on the lid of the opposite sarcophagus and began to work it open. It scraped and screeched until I'd managed to get it as far off as possible without it falling off the side. I grimaced at the sound and listened carefully for either Maggie's warning or the shout of a security guard. Taking a deep breath, I snatched up the Maglite and shone it inside.

The draugr lay peacefully in repose, arms stretched out at its side. It looked like a fairly ordinary corpse at first glance, but a closer look revealed that the flesh clinging to its bones was far too robust, the skin almost pink rather than black with age. An inexperienced eye would claim that the body laying before them had only been dead a short time, not a hundred and fifty years.

It says here, Maggie intoned, *that draugr raised by a powerful necromancer are impossible to kill permanently unless you find their resting place.*

What the hell are you reading from?

It's called The Weary Dead, *and it's by some court physician. Fourteenth century, I think. It says that draugr will grow in strength each time you destroy its physical form. By virtue of its master's magic, it will reassemble itself in its grave and become stronger and stronger each time it does so. By the third time it rises—which will be in a couple of days—its flesh will appear almost human, and it will have access to black magic, including shapeshifting, the force of wind, and control over lesser animals.*

Okay, then. We should kill it ASAP.

Stop interrupting; I'm almost finished. The draugr's fury will increase each time it is destroyed, blah-blah-blah, and it will stop at nothing to accomplish its master's will so that it may be released to terrorize the world. Huh.

So that explains why they tried to kill me even with Nick being locked up and out of the picture.

Yup.

All right, let's do this. I leaned over, wooden stake in one hand, and tapped the draugr on the forehead. It didn't move. *You sure it's not getting up?*

Not until we make it.

Good. I set aside the stake and picked up the cord, reaching underneath the lid to feel with one hand along the draugr's shin, ankle, and foot. I grasped him first by one big toe, then by the other. *This is really gross*, I said.

You're fine. It's just an undead body.

Undead bodies are gross.

Maggie began to hum the way she does when she's absently flipping through the pages of a book. *Hey, this is cool. John D. Rockefeller is buried here.*

The oil tycoon? I asked.

One and the same.

No kidding. Jesus, this is hard to tie.

The guy who invented the Salisbury steak is buried here too.

I should stop and pay my respects. I ate nothing but microwave dinners for most of my childhood.

That explains a lot.

What the hell is that supposed to mean? Ah! Got it. I successfully finished looping the cord around the draugr's toes and tied a one-handed knot before extricating myself from the sarcophagus and dusting off the sleeve of my hoodie. I took the iron ingot and laid it on the draugr's chest. *What now?*

Now we wake him up.

A cord and a piece of iron are gonna keep him from trying to rip my face off again?

We should need only one of them, but I figured insurance wasn't a bad idea.

You know he has hands, right? He can just untie the cord and move the ingot.

Not according to this. Trust me, this kind of thing works on all sorts of Other.

Man, magic sure is dumb sometimes, I said. I took one of the bags of draugr dust and sprinkled it on the body—along with bits of my ruined truck and some road gravel—then took Maggie's ring and pressed the ruby against the draugr's forehead.

The draugr immediately took a long gasp, like a man coming up for air after a long dive. It began to tremble violently, rasping and hissing, and I leapt back against its brother's sarcophagi and let the creature thrash. Thanks to the narrow width of its resting place, it was able to do little more than flail its bony arms upward. I pointed my Maglite at it and took a cautious look inside to see that it indeed remained pinned to the sarcophagus floor by the iron. Its eyes fixed on the flashlight. Eyes. Those were new.

"Hey, big guy, how you doing?"

"Release me," it demanded in a gravelly voice.

Well, at least it can talk.

That's good and bad, Maggie said. *Good because it can answer questions. Bad because it shouldn't be able to talk until after it's been destroyed three times.*

So your book may or may not be accurate. Great. The iron is holding it down, at least.

"Damn you, release me!" it repeated.

I glanced outside. "Hey, pal, keep it down unless you want a security guard on top of us."

"I will kill you and anyone who comes."

"Sure, sure. Until OtherOps calls in a SWAT team. You don't want to deal with that." I shone my light on the sarcophagus lid. "Listen, Trevor, I just need you and your brother to answer one question, and then I'll do exactly what you ask."

Draugr Trevor went still and glared at me. "I only answer

to one mortal."

"Right, Nick the Necromancer. I just need to know who hired Nick."

"Hired him for what?"

"To get the jinn from me."

"I have nothing to say to you."

I cocked an eyebrow at the creature. It was, truthfully, more than a little terrifying. It and its brother had almost killed me the other day. But watching it lie there and flail its arms, unable to do something as simple as lift a piece of iron off its chest, made me crack a smile. "That iron—does it hurt?"

"It burns," Trevor hissed.

"I could just put the roof back on your little house here and leave you to cook under that iron for the next few weeks. How would you like that?"

It made a strange sound in the back of its throat. "I know little of value."

"Tell me what I want to know, and I'll release you. Cross my heart."

Its arm trembled, and I wondered what kind of horrible things it was imagining doing to me the moment it could get out of that sarcophagus. "Master..."

"Nick?"

"Yes, Nick. He spoke with her on the tel... tel..."

"Telephone? Who's *her*?"

"A woman. We went to her home. It was a large, white house. Perhaps a mansion?"

"What was her name?"

"I did not hear it."

"So where was the house?"

"It was in a place..." Trevor hesitated for a moment, and then his eyebrows rose. "Ah. The rich man. It is the land where he used to live."

I leaned on the edge of the sarcophagi and eyed Trevor's

hands. I had no doubt he'd snatch for me, given the opportunity. "You need to be more specific."

"The tycoon. I don't remember his name."

"Rockefeller?"

"Yes!"

"Huh." *Where did he used to live?* I asked Maggie.

I'm sure we can find out.

I considered this for a moment, digging through my memories of local history. I snapped my fingers. "Cleveland Heights! Gotta be it. So a white mansion in Cleveland Heights. That's not super useful, but it's a start. Is that all you've got?" I asked Trevor.

"It's all I know. Now release me!"

"Here's the thing," I said, and brought the wooden stake up over my head and buried it between Trevor's ribs. The draugr let out a wild moan, its claws tearing my sleeves to ribbons as it grasped at me. *Maggie, a little help.* The ring flared, and fire shot down through the stake and washed across the draugr's bones, consuming it in moments. By the time I righted myself, there was nothing left of the corpse but ash. My wooden stake remained undamaged, and I retrieved the cord and iron. *Is he gone for good this time?*

Should be.

See, the word should *does not help me sleep at night.*

Would you prefer I lie to you and say, "Yes, I am one hundred percent certain we killed that draugr"?

Yes, I think I would.

I pushed the lid back on the sarcophagus and gathered my equipment before going through the exact same process with Trevor's undead brother. Ten minutes later, with nothing more to go on than the information Trevor had given us, I climbed the wall out of Lake View Cemetery and headed back to my rental car. I turned on the radio, volume low, and listened to Paul Simon's "American Tune" while I meditated on the events of the past week. The draugr hadn't been as helpful as I'd hoped, which meant I still needed to get Nick to talk. There was no telling how long he'd be able to hold out. With the clock ticking on Ferryman's job, I wasn't exactly flush with spare time—but with someone out there trying to get Maggie's ring, I couldn't just put it off.

I put my chair back and closed my eyes. *Wake me up in two hours, please,* I said to Maggie.

What's in two hours?

Presti's opens. An hour after that, the morning shift arrives at the OtherOps office.

CHAPTER 11

I was waiting at the door to the Cleveland OtherOps offices when the day shift arrived—nine men and women wearing either sharp black suits or OtherOps polos and black slacks. They were laughing at a joke someone had made as they approached the building, carrying their morning coffees. The laughter broke off when they spotted me, and one of them disengaged from the group and approached.

Justin Hamilton was in his midthirties and had been with OtherOps for over a decade. If he weren't such a nice guy, I'd probably hate his guts. He was tall, thin, black-haired and svelte, with movie-star cheekbones. He had that kind of easy smile that makes Maggie go *ooh* every time we see him. We met before he joined OtherOps—back when Ada enrolled me in jujitsu as a teenager so I would be more useful to her.

We've been friends ever since, even though I don't actually get to see him that often. Most OtherOps agents will do anything to fuck with reapers. They resent us because we're better-paid independent contractors who can get away with murder. We resent them because they have better work hours, government job security, and can get away with murder. Justin and I have never had that issue. I do the occasional favor for the local OtherOps office, and in exchange, his boss gives him quite a lot of leniency when I ask for information that a regular cop would definitely get in trouble for handing out.

We shook hands, and he gave me that damned smile, even though it was eight AM. I was running on less than two hours of sleep, so my response came out as a grimace. "What are you doin' here so early?" he asked, looking at his watch. "We're a little too old to have beer for breakfast."

"Are we?" I joked, following him inside after the rest of the day shift had gone ahead. "We do need to set up that drink. Next Thursday?"

"I'll make the time if you will."

"Barring an emergency…"

Justin rolled his eyes. He doesn't know *exactly* what my circumstances are with Ada, but he suspects them. One of the reasons we get along so well is because he doesn't take it personally when I cancel on him at the last moment in favor of work. Other than the seven-hundred-year-old jinn on my finger, Justin is my only actual friend. Which, on its own, is kind of depressing.

"Yeah, yeah," he said. "Cork and Bottle?"

"Sounds good to me. Hey, did you follow up on that meth house full of dead imps?"

"Follow up on it?" he asked, swiping an ID badge and holding the door open for me. "We brought in a whole team from Columbus to sort through that mess. They were working all night."

"Any idea what killed the imps?"

He shook his head. "We sent a few samples to the lab, but that shit takes forever to process. Our best guesses were a werewolf or a wendigo."

"But neither of them really fits."

"Exactly." Justin waved hello to one of the night shift and set his coffee on his desk, then leaned against the wall of his cubicle. "Could have been damn well anything. There're Others out there that we know next to nothing about, so when something like this happens, we sort through the usual suspects first, then head to the more obscure."

"Let me know if you get anything," I said. A secretary squeezed between us with an "Excuse me," and I caught one of the junior OtherOps agents staring at me from two cubicles over. I tend to stand out in a room full of black suits and smart polos. I gave him a toothy grin, and he quickly looked down.

Justin crossed his arms. "So are you going to tell me what

all this is about? First you ask me to run an ID on a picture of a dead imp, then a whole meth crew winds up dead at the address I give you."

"Not sure if they're related," I lied.

"Not sure, huh?" Justin asked skeptically. "Where'd you get that picture?"

"Sorry, client confidentiality."

Justin snorted. "If I were a cop, I'd be suspicious."

"If you were a cop, I'd be sitting in a little room with two of your detectives and a lawyer right now. Lucky for me, you're not." I threw up my hands. "Look, if I come across anything that falls under OtherOps purview, you'll be my first phone call."

"Unless your clients ask you not to call me," he retorted.

Justin is, if you haven't been able to tell, far too clever for his own good.

He asked, "Did you come all the way out here at this hour just to ask me about that? You could have called."

"Not exactly," I said. "Do you still have that necromancer in lockup?"

"Sure I do. He refuses a lawyer and won't tell us what he's after or who he is. We know nothing about him or his motives. Until we do, he stays under lock and key."

A thought struck me. "Do you think that *he* thinks someone is going to let him out of here?"

"No idea. Don't particularly care. I'm not a fan of punk kids with a pile of talent and no discipline. Another week or two, and we'll send him to the pen in New York. He won't be my problem anymore, which suits me fine."

I nodded along, trying to figure out what this necromancer kid gained by staying silent. Coming up with nothing, I said, "This is going to sound like an odd request, but can I talk to him?"

Justin raised one eyebrow. "Not against any rules as far as I know. Be my guest."

"Alone. No cameras. No microphones."

"Oh, come on. You can't seriously ask that after a whole bunch of imps wound up dead with you at the scene. We know you didn't do it, of course, but your name is still on the report for a massacre."

"I'm not going to kill him," I protested. "I just want to see if he'll talk to me when no one's listening."

Justin sighed and made a dismissive gesture. "I've got to get to work. You do whatever you want to do. Just don't beat the shit out of him or anything. The guys up top smile favorably on you for that bunyip business, but they'll stop smiling if you rough up a perp. Our suppression team will be just outside if you need them."

Five minutes later, I sat behind an empty desk in a small white room buried in one corner of the OtherOps building. It had a single fluorescent light and no windows, and I imagined it was the place they sent new hires who hadn't yet been given a cubicle. I took a few moments to consider my next move on Ferryman's case. I knew I couldn't waste any more time on this necromancer business than I already had. I'd have to hit the pavement again the moment this meeting was over.

None of it made sense. Murdering the imps to cover up the secondhand soul business was the move of an amateur. If they were trying to bury the whole thing, adding a pile of bodies would do little more than attract OtherOps' attention. But if whoever was doing this had access to a creature that Maggie couldn't pin down, they weren't an amateur.

And then there was Ferryman. Whoever stole those souls had to know that Ferryman would get involved eventually, and he's about the only thing in the Other who will scare literally everyone. Were we dealing with someone who was insane? Stupid? Arrogant? All of the above?

I tucked all those thoughts away for later as the door opened and Nick the Necromancer was led inside by a pair of very large individuals in tactical vests. They shoved him into the chair across from me, shot me a single glance, and retreated into the hallway, where I got a glimpse of an elderly woman with crosses tattooed on her face.

At the sight of her, I felt Maggie stir in the back of my head. *Is that the suppression team?* I asked her.

It is. She's a magician—damn good one too. Our buddy Nick might be powerful, but I bet she'd turn him into a pretzel given the chance.

Can she sense your presence? I asked in alarm.

If she can, she hasn't tried to say hello. I've spent five hundred and twenty-three years making sure this ring is hidden from people like her, so I doubt she'll be a problem.

Right. Let's hope she doesn't decide to take a closer look. That's another thing reapers get jealous of OtherOps agents for: when they need serious firepower, they get it. I mentally cussed out Ferryman once again for bringing his problem to me rather than the people with access to a genuine army.

I turned my attention to Nick and plastered a pleasant smile on my face. "Hiya, Nick. How's the food?"

Nick slumped petulantly in his seat, the stainless steel chain of his restraints jangling. "What the hell do you want?"

"Just thought I'd stop by and say hi. See how the ol' jumpsuit is fitting. Orange really doesn't suit you, ya know?" Inwardly, I asked Maggie, *Is the magician listening in?*

As far as I can tell, they're giving us privacy.

Nick looked over his shoulder at the closed door, then at me. "You put down my draugr, didn't you?"

"I did," I responded, covering up my surprise. I was no expert on magic, but the fact he was being guarded by a suppression team yet could still sense when his familiars were destroyed was pretty impressive. "Tracked them to Lake View and put a stake through their hearts. The assholes wrecked my truck, you know. Not happy about that."

I expected him to come back with some sort of threat, but instead he slumped farther down in his seat and watched me carefully. After a few moments of silence, he said, "How did you do it? You're just a troll. You're tough, but you don't have any magic. You..." He stopped, chewed on a fingernail, and went on. "It was the jinn, wasn't it? You carry her with you. It's in the ring."

It wasn't a question, and I didn't bother to answer. I leaned forward. "Tell me who you're working for, Nick."

"I will not."

"Why not?"

"Because I made a vow of silence when I took the job."

Is he telling the truth? I asked Maggie.

He is.

I snorted. "Why would you do a thing like that?"

"For this eventuality."

"For a kid, you sure do plan well. Or was it your boss's idea?"

"It was her idea. And I'm not a kid. I'm nineteen."

"That's a kid in this line of work," I told him. "Most people consider *me* a kid, and I've been at this for twenty years." I stood up, stretching until my arms touched the walls, and looked down at Nick with a tight smile. "So you either won't or can't tell me anything. That means you're useless to me."

Nick sat up suddenly. "What does that mean?"

"Exactly what it sounds like," I told him. "You tried to kill me in broad daylight, and your familiars wrecked my truck. I don't like you, Nick, and somehow I don't think you're going to pay for a new truck. Add on top of that the fact that I'd prefer to keep you quiet about the jinn, and you're in a tight spot."

You just confirmed you have my ring, Maggie sniffed. *I hope you're going somewhere good with this.*

Hang in there with me.

Nick looked toward the door. "All I have to do is scream."

I laughed. "You think I'd kill you in person?" I made a show of twirling Maggie's ring. "Nah. I'll give you twenty-four hours to come up with something good to tell me, and then..." I shrugged.

Nick swallowed.

He's doing that thing where he looks more like a stupid, scared teenager than a powerful necromancer, Maggie said. *Almost makes me feel bad. You are aware that I can't actually kill him like that, right?*

He doesn't have to know I'm bluffing, I told her. I patted Nick on the shoulder and knocked on the door. "I'm done," I told the suppression team outside.

I found Justin at his cubicle, answering emails. He didn't look up as I leaned over the cubicle wall and took a peanut butter cup out of the little jar by his keyboard. "Get anything out of the kid?" he asked me.

"Nothing. He claims that he made a vow of silence to his employer. Which could mean all sorts of things, but I'm inclined to believe him."

"Should I go ahead and just send him to New York?" Justin asked.

I took another peanut butter cup and tapped it on the top of Justin's monitor thoughtfully. "No. Keep him around. He'll probably ask for a phone call soon. When he does, tap the line and let me know who he calls."

"I'm not sure if I'm allowed to do that," Justin said, finally looking up from his computer.

"Not sure, or definitely not allowed?"

"Not sure."

"Better to ask forgiveness than permission," I said with a smile.

He rolled his eyes. "You realize that you're buying, like, the next ten weeks' worth of drinks, right?"

"Now, now, let's talk price once we've actually found out who's trying to have me killed."

I said goodbye and headed back to my rental, where I took a few moments to close my eyes in the quiet darkness of the parking garage. I could feel Maggie pacing around in the back of my head. I had almost fallen asleep when she spoke. *Scaring him into calling his employer is clever.*

Glad you think so.

If it works. He's a smart kid.

True, but most people think that OtherOps are like cops and won't bug your phones or detain you without reason and bullshit like that.

Aren't you afraid that he'll just tell his handlers what he was after? Magicians really *like getting their hands on magical baubles, and I bet that one in the OtherOps office wouldn't hesitate to confiscate me.*

You can't be confiscated without killing me.

You think that would stop her? Magicians are amoral twats.

I sighed. It was an alarming suggestion, to be sure, and I hoped I was as clever as I liked to think I was. *He's under a vow of silence. He literally can't tell anyone about the ring.* I hope, I added in a thought Maggie couldn't hear.

There was a pause. *Okay, I'll give you credit for that one.*

Thanks, I said. I was a little worried that I had tipped my hand about the ring so easily. He knew it was on my finger now, which meant if he managed to escape he could just kill me from a distance and take the damn thing. *I had a thought while we were in there. Stop me if this sounds ridiculous.*

Go for it.

Back at the cemetery, you mentioned how draugr can become shapeshifters as they become more powerful.

Yeah.

On Ferryman's case, could we be dealing with a shapeshifter?

We already ruled out werewolves and wendigos.

No, I said, *not a man who can become a creature—a genuine shapeshifter.*

Maggie seemed to consider the idea. *Why do you say that?*

Because it's the only thing I can think of that checks all the boxes: shapeshifters, like undead, are hard to identify with sorcery. OtherOps didn't have a ready ID on whatever killed those imps. And everything I've heard about shapeshifters is that the constant switching between manifestations leaves them unhinged, which you have to be to move in on Ferryman's turf.

Huh, she responded. *I buy it. But there's over a hundred varieties of shapeshifter out there, and they're all stupidly rare. What are we looking for?*

No idea. But I have another idea.

Yeah?

It's really stupid.

Oh, no.

I shook the sleep out of my head and started the car. *I'm going to poke it with a stick until it decides to come out and play.*

Chapter 12

The first thing I did was make a phone call to Zeke. The retired cherubim picked up on the fifth ring, answering with a groggy, "Hello."

"Morning, Zeke. I need you to do something for me."

"Alek? What time is it? It's... oh, Christ, it's nine in the morning. Call me back in three hours."

"If you hang up," I said pleasantly, "I'm going to drive down there and kick the shit out of you."

That seemed to wake him up. His voice sobered instantly—cautious, with a dangerous inflection to it. Not a lot of people threaten angels, retired or not. "What's going on, Alek?" he demanded.

I held the phone with my shoulder and ordered breakfast at a Chick-fil-A drive-through. "You still there?" I asked him.

"Yes, I'm still here. What do you want?"

"I want the address of every imp meth house in northeast Ohio."

There was a long, pregnant pause. I could just imagine the confused look on Zeke's face as he processed the request. "*If* I had that kind of information, it wouldn't come cheap," he finally said.

"I'm pretty sure you do have that kind of information," I retorted, "and you're going to give it to me for free, or you're never going to get work from me or anyone at Valkyrie Collections ever again."

"Whoa, whoa! What's gotten into you, man? Why the hell would you say something like that?"

I let my exhaustion and irritation bleed into my voice. After being stonewalled by a teenage necromancer, I didn't have patience for Zeke. "Because you sold me to that necromancer."

Another pause. "I, uh, don't know what you're talking about."

"He told me it was you, twit. His draugr almost killed me twice, and they smashed up my truck. I'm driving around in a goddamn rented Prius and I'm pretty pissed off about it, so if you want to remain my go-to guy when Ada's looking to spread around the bribe money, you're going to get me those address."

"I might be able to dig something up by next week."

"You've got twenty minutes," I said. "Ticktock." I hung up and pulled into a parking spot, where I ate my breakfast slowly and downed four cups of fast-food coffee. I'd just finished picking the crumbs off my shirt when my phone buzzed. It was an email from Zeke, and it contained eight different addresses and a note at the bottom that said, *This is Kappie's territory. If he catches you snooping around, I had nothing to do with this.* I made a quick mental map of the addresses, working clockwise around Cleveland, and typed the first address into my GPS.

Do you think this is a good idea? Maggie asked.

Not really. If it doesn't draw him out, I'll have wasted my entire day. If it does...

Then you'll probably get killed by a shapeshifter.

That's why I have you here, I said.

I'm not a fan of going after creatures we know nothing about. If it is a shapeshifter, it could be anything from a goblin wizard to an ancient trickster god. One of those is out of our league. I'll let you guess which.

The first address was actually less than ten minutes from Valkyrie HQ, on a cul-de-sac in Euclid. At first glance, the place was abandoned—the windows boarded up, the roof in disrepair, the driveway cracked and full of weeds. But there were two cars parked in the cul-de-sac, and as I scoped the place out, I watched an emaciated imp walk past with a little mutt cattle dog on an extension cord as a makeshift leash. The dog stopped in the driveway and threw up bile before the imp dragged it around behind the house.

"Prick," I said aloud. I got out of the car and strapped on my holster and flak vest, then put on a hat with the Valkyrie company logo on the front. I didn't bother with a jacket, despite the chill spring weather. Because of my troll blood, my arms look like I work out a whole lot, and I wanted to show them off in short sleeves. The display of force was for a couple reasons: first, because low-level imps tend to be sniveling cowards who will cow before an immediate threat; and second, because if this hypothetical shapeshifting creature showed up to tumble, I wanted it to think my gun and vest were the only surprises I had ready for him.

How we looking? I asked Maggie.

Four imps inside. Another two out back.

I ignored the front door and walked around the side, following the imp with the dog, only to find him and a friend standing by the back door. They poured a can of beer into a bowl and laughed while the dog slurped it up hungrily.

"Beer is bad for dogs," I said flatly.

Both imps leapt out of their skin. They turned on me and froze, sharing a single glance.

"I'm not a cop," I added quickly.

The two imps looked so much alike that they might have been twins. One wore a red sweater—probably a thrift store find—and the other a T-shirt with the slogan of a failed presidential campaign from six years ago. Red Sweater nudged his friend and lifted his chin toward my gun. "If you're not a cop, who are you?"

"Alek Fitz. I'm a reaper."

"Reapers ain't got shit on us, man," T-shirt spat at me, his initial fear turning to posturing.

I walked over to the two and gently took the bowl of beer away from the dog, tossing it over the nearby fence.

"Hey!" T-shirt began.

I grabbed him by the chin and squeezed a little. "You—

walk to the store and get two cans of *good* dog food. And a real leash."

"I'm not—" he tried to say.

I squeezed until he let out a high-pitched squeal. "I'm not a cop. I don't mind hurting you. Good dog food and a leash. Got it?"

"Yeah, yeah!"

I let him go, and he sprinted off around the side of the house. I tilted my head, listening to make sure that he continued down the sidewalk instead of going in the front door. When I was satisfied he was gone, I said to his friend, "I'm looking for someone."

Red Sweater shied away from me. "If you're looking for an imp, you've got to take it up with Kappie. I just work here."

"I don't want to talk to Kappie. I want to talk to the peons. Some of your friends have been taking work on the side—stuff Kappie didn't give them. I want you to tell me what you know."

Red Sweater's eyes grew large. "Shit, man, Kappie's the big guy. We go against him, and we're fucked."

I don't think he has any idea what you're talking about, Maggie said.

"I'm looking for the person offering these side jobs," I continued.

"We wouldn't . . ."

I cut him off. "The employer is either scarier or paying better than Kappie. Maybe both. I don't really give a shit. Do you know Kappie's cookhouse out in Ashtabula?"

He gave a dumb nod.

"Do you know what happened?"

Red Sweater licked his lips. "Heard there was some kind of a gunfight. Everybody ended up dead."

"That what Kappie told you?"

"Yeah…"

I put my hand on his shoulder. The little creep was barely

more than skin and bone. I spoke in a low, gentle tone. "What really happened is that almost a dozen imps got torn to pieces. *Pieces.* They were working for the thing that did it to them, and I'm on its trail." With one hand, I produced a card from my pocket and put it in his hand. "I want you to call around to all your friends and cousins. You tell 'em that something is killing imps. Your boss doesn't care, but I do. If any of them tell you a story about a stranger offering work, you call me immediately."

The imp stared at my card for a few moments, then looked up at me. I could see him summoning courage. "What's in it for me?" he asked.

Oh, for fuck's sake, I said to Maggie. *It's almost like not getting killed isn't enough.* "You find me this asshole, and I'll give you five hundred bucks, plus another hundred for whoever your source is." I leaned forward so that we were eye to eye. "*After* I get my hands on the guy. Got it?"

"Right. Got it. Yes, sir."

I opened the back door, covering my mouth against the eye-watering stench of ammonia. Four imps sat on bare, stained carpet watching an old tube TV. Two of them got to their feet as I entered. "Sit down," I said. "I don't give a shit what you're cooking in here." I produced a handful of business cards and gave them each the same spiel and offer I'd given their red-sweatered friend, then went back outside as quickly as I could manage.

I hocked up a wad of phlegm, spat in the dirt, and rubbed my eyes. "How the hell do you guys breathe in there?"

"We wear masks when we're cooking," Red Sweater replied.

"And the rest of the time?"

He shrugged.

I looked down at the little cattle dog and chewed on the inside of my cheek. It stared up at me expectantly, clearly disappointed I had taken its breakfast. It inched forward and licked the tips of my fingers.

We don't have time for this, Maggie warned.

I took the extension cord out of Red Sweater's hand. "I'm confiscating your dog."

"Hey!"

"Don't keep pets in a meth house," I called over my shoulder as I left.

I went out of my way to drop the dog at a nearby shelter whose owner owed me a favor, then headed to the next address on Zeke's list. It was much the same as the first: occupied by a handful of imps who cooked meth for Kappie. The imps protested that no one would accept work without Kappie's allowance, but they all ate up my promise of a five-hundred-dollar bounty for this mysterious employer.

The third house followed suit, and the fourth and the fifth. It was getting late in the afternoon when I reached the sixth house, in a town called Berea. I pulled into the driveway, and Maggie immediately chimed in. *Don't bother. The house is empty.*

Completely?

Completely, she confirmed. *Kappie must have cleaned it out months ago.*

I sighed. *This isn't working, is it?*

Before Maggie could answer, my phone rang. It was an unidentified number. "Alek Fitz," I answered.

A nasally voice said, "Are you the reaper guy?"

"Yeah, that's me." I thought I recognized the voice of Red Sweater from the Euclid house. "Do you have anything for me?"

"Maybe," he answered. "My cousin's friend is helping open up a cook house over in Painesville. He says some spooky dude offered them a side job, but he wouldn't say what it was."

"That's not super specific," I said.

"Hey, man, that's all I've got. Do I get the five hundred bucks or what?"

I checked Zeke's list. No houses in Painesville. "Text me the address," I told him. "If it's a good lead, you'll get your money when I drag this sucker down."

The address arrived on my phone within thirty seconds, and I was on my way to Painesville. It was dark by the time I pulled up in front of a little cottage on a two-acre lot that still had a realtor's sign out front. Someone had spray-painted BLACK MOLD on the realtor's sign. There were three cars in the driveway, the lawn was unkempt, and I could see light coming from around the edges of blacked-out windows.

It didn't take a lot of effort to bully my way inside and corral seven imps onto the two beat-up couches in the living room. I stood in the middle of the room, looking at the seven as if I were about to give a presentation. Not a single one gave me trouble beyond asking who I was, but they all fixed me with the same hollow-eyed look I had seen on the guy back in Euclid. Something was most definitely wrong here, though. "Five hundred bucks," I said firmly, hoping to get a rise. "First one of you who sells out your boss gets it in cash."

"Kappie's our boss," one answered.

"Your other boss," I clarified.

One of the imps, a younger one with a hairlip, looked around at his friends before opening his mouth. "I—" His closest companion punched him in the shoulder, and he fell silent.

"You what?" I asked, walking over to stand above him.

We came to the right place, Maggie told me.

You sure?

They're all scared shitless. They're practically exhaling fear.

"Come on," I said. "Five hundred bucks to the first one to speak." I did a circuit around the room, then returned to Hairlip and nudged his shoe with my boot. "Five hundred not good enough? You guys need some group courage? How about two hundred each?"

Still no rise. I straightened, scowling at the assembled imps. *It's like they think he's going to show up any second,* I said to Maggie.

About that, Alek—you have company.

You're shitting me. Where?

Outside, coming quick.

I drew my Glock and backed into the corner of the living room, one eye on the front door and the other on the window. The imps stared at me in confusion. *Where is he?* I asked Maggie.

I'm trying to figure that out! I can't pin the bastard down; he's—

Maggie was cut off by a deafening rumble. It felt like a concrete truck driving by at full speed, and I tried to pinpoint the source with no more luck than Maggie when I heard a snap, felt a breeze on my neck, and something snagged the back of my flak vest all in the course of a split second. The word *shit* wasn't out of my mouth when I felt myself yanked *through* the wall of the house, crunching through the drywall, framing, and siding. I was suddenly tumbling through the air. I instinctively curled into a ball a moment before I bounced off a tree and went skidding across the muddy yard to land in a heap about twenty yards from the house.

Alek!

I'm awake! I responded, pulling myself gingerly to my knees. My lower back—where I'd hit the tree—felt like I'd been hit by a wrecking ball. The rest of me ached so badly that my fingers tingled. I remembered the house, then remembered my gun, then remembered that something very angry was on its way to eat me. I used every ounce of concentration to get to my feet. *Gun?* I asked Maggie.

Eight feet to your left. Yes, there.

A scream pierced the night as I recovered my weapon. It was followed by another, and the screams soon erupted into a chorus. I swung toward the house, watching in horror through the hole in the wall as *something* tore through those imps as easily as I would a box of pet-store bunnies. *Why isn't he coming after me? Why is he... shit, he's killing my witnesses!* I broke into a sprint, ignoring the pain in my side. I checked the Glock, not bothering to close more than half the distance before I pulled up, braced myself, and squeezed off two quick shots.

The screaming went silent, and the shadows inside the house went still. I approached slowly, gun raised. *I didn't kill it, did I?*

I don't think so... Maggie sounded uncertain.

I reached the corner of the house and eyeballed the spot where the creature had snatched me and pulled me through. He must have gone in the same way, because the hole was quite a bit larger than I was. Inside, the living room light had been shattered, and the room was illuminated by a knocked-over lamp and light coming in from the kitchen. *Is it gone?*

Maggie didn't answer.

Carefully, I climbed up into the living room. I cleared it, then the kitchen and back bedroom before returning to the living room and taking in the carnage. It was the same as in Ashtabula—corpses lay like discarded rag dolls, some of them separated from limbs and heads. Bellies were torn open; throats were cut. The killing had no pattern beyond whatever was quick and convenient. Blood spatter covered the walls and ceilings, and blood still spurted from one headless body.

A sickly cough brought my gun back up. I spun toward the front door, where I was surprised to find Hairlip lying halfway behind the television, one leg skiwampus with the bone sticking out, using both hands to hold in his intestines. I swallowed my bile and knelt next to him, pulling out my phone and hitting record on the camera. "That thing," I said. "That's what you were afraid of?"

Hairlip's eyes were closed. He let out a whimper.

"Do you know who or what it is?" I said. "Does it have a name?"

Alek.

I know it's shitty, but I need to know, I told Maggie.

It's not that. Back up slowly. Do it now. Hairlip's real body is on the other side of the room.

Hairlip's eyes shot open. My first thought was that they were bright yellow, like a cat's, and my second was to throw myself backward as Hairlip's body shimmered and twisted, one enormous, mangy, taloned hand shooting toward me with the speed of a striking adder. The talons snagged in my flak vest, and the strength of the creature threw me sideways into the wall. Grendel's claw flared to life on my left hand, and I brought my hand down hard in a karate chop, using the power of the tattoo to sever the shapeshifter's hand at the wrist.

The shapeshifter recoiled, letting out a strange, warbling scream as it finished shifting from Hairlip into a something that looked like the fuckchild of a rabid werewolf and an excavator. Even with its shoulders hunched, its head dragged along the ceiling. It took one step back, let out a howl, and drew its long, black tongue across the bloody stump at the end of its arm.

Without a second thought, I emptied the rest of my Glock into it.

The shapeshifter fell back several more steps, grunting as the bullets traced crimson flowers across its chest. The impacts barely seemed to have any affect, and I braced myself for the thing to leap at me, jaws snapping. It seemed to shimmer again, growing smaller even as it leapt toward the window.

"God damn it," I said as I ran toward the front door.

By the time I was outside, all I could see was the tail of something catlike disappearing into the underbrush far faster than I could ever hope to give chase. And I had no interest in chasing a shapeshifter in the dark through unfamiliar woods. I waited for several minutes on the front lawn until Maggie gave me the all clear. I stumbled back inside.

You're bleeding.

I touched the side of my head. My fingers came away crimson. *That thing hits like a truck*, I told Maggie. *Fast as hell too.* I carefully crossed the room, looking for my phone, and found it between Hairlip's real head and the severed foot of one of his companions. I wiped the imp blood from my phone onto my torn-up flak vest and replayed the video I was in the middle of taking when the shapeshifter revealed itself. I saw the yellow eyes and the swiping of the claw, and then the phone got thrown across the room when I went into the wall. It had landed at an angle, catching a good shot of the creature's head as the sound of my Glock cracked sharply in the background.

I turned off the video. Sitting on my haunches, surrounded by bodies, I ran my hand over my face. My hand brushed across my tusks, and I let out a tired little laugh. I hadn't even felt them emerge. I willed them back to normal, ignoring the pain in my gums to focus on the pain running down my side. Such a hit would have probably paralyzed a normal person—maybe even killed them outright. I'd feel lucky if X-rays didn't show a couple of cracked ribs.

What do you want to bet that our shapeshifter has either already killed or is on his way to kill anyone else who's worked for him? I asked Maggie. I got up and walked into the kitchen, looking across a bunch of meth-making equipment that didn't look like it had been used yet. I glanced through the cupboards, then walked into the back bedroom and opened the top drawer of a dresser. Staring back at me in the drawer were at least a dozen soul mirrors. *Well, that's a start*, I said, gathering them up. *He didn't have time to grab these before he took off.* I paused, listening for some reply. *Maggie?*

Yeah, I'm here, she replied distractedly.

What's wrong?

Nothing. I'm trying to read.

Well, you picked a damn strange time to do it.
Research, dummy.

I checked the rest of the drawers, then underneath the beds and in the closet. All in all, I left the house with almost thirty soul mirrors. I tossed them in the Prius's trunk, got in the car, and started driving. I hadn't been on the road long when my phone rang.

"Hey, Alek, it's Nadine."

"You still at work?"

"I am. Still digging through that file on Judith Pyke."

To be honest, I'd completely forgotten about it. I perked up. "Anything useful?"

"Not sure. Just a random tidbit I found."

"What's that?"

"Judith herself might not even know, but the offices she rents downtown are all owned by Kappie Shuteye."

"Huh. Anything else?"

"Not yet. I'll let you know."

I hung up and drove in silence, considering this new bit of information for several minutes, unsure of which direction I wanted to take this. Tying Kappie to Judith could mean Kappie was involved... or it could just mean that whoever was using Kappie's muscle also had access to his more legitimate records, like rental tenants. I was almost back to the office when Maggie broke into my thoughts.

I've got it, she said.

Got what?

What we're dealing with.

That's good?

No. No, it's not.

I cleared my throat. *Trickster god?*

Not quite. It's a ghoul.

You mean one of those things you were telling me about the other day?

Yeah. Maggie sighed. *You don't want to be driving when I tell you about this.*

Chapter 13

I stood by Ferryman's card table in his realm of darkness, watching while he carefully placed an eight on top of a nine. The thirty recovered soul mirrors sat on the table beside him. He ashed his cigarette absently on one, then seemed to notice what he had done and gently blew the ash off of it. He moved a queen of diamonds and finally peered up at me.

"Well done," he said, tapping one long fingernail on a soul mirror. "Where are the rest?"

"A thank-you would be nice," I replied.

"Thank you," he said flatly. "Where are the rest?"

I took out my phone and set it in front of him, pressing play on the video I took the night before. He watched it in silence and, once it had finished, tapped the phone to watch it again. He leaned back, gazing up at me thoughtfully.

"I think it's a ghoul," I told him.

"Certainly a shapeshifter," he said. I could have sworn that his eyes darted ever-so-quickly toward Maggie's ring. "A ghoul seems likely," he amended. "An undead desert spirit. What the hell is it doing in Cleveland?"

"Selling secondhand souls, apparently. It's the twenty-first century. Gotta go where business is, right?" I've met enough Other not to bother questioning their motivations. They like money and power just as much as—and often more than—any human.

Ferryman shrugged. "I can't argue with that. I don't like the undead—zombies, vampires, what have you." He made a dismissive gesture. "Whoever makes them does so in direct mockery of me without breaking the Rules. Ghouls are some of the worst. Some god created them way back in…" He seemed to search his memory, then gave up. "The worst thing about undead is that they don't fear me anymore, and that's just unhealthy."

Maggie had spent the better part of last night telling me everything about ghouls she either knew already or could glean from her library. From what she'd said, their lack of fear was not the worst thing about them—not even close. Ghouls were powerfully strong in whatever form they chose to take. They were fast, malicious, cruel, and possessed a cunning that allowed them to stay two steps ahead of anyone trying to follow their rampages.

I leaned over Ferryman's card table and tapped on my phone. "*That* is way above my pay grade." I took a map of northeast Ohio out of my pocket and set it in front of him. I used a pen to circle the locations of the Ashtabula and Painesville meth houses. "He hired imps here and there. Now, ghouls need grave dirt to recharge during twilight hours. I'm willing to bet if you got yourself an OtherOps sweep team and told them exactly what they were looking for, they'd be able to search every graveyard in two counties, starting with these locations, and you could have your asshole ghoul in three or four days."

Ferryman didn't bother to look at the map. "Are you scared of it?" he asked.

"Are you joking? That thing could be thousands of years old. I'm a twenty-eight-year-old mixed-blood troll. I can throw around imps and humans without a problem. I could probably go toe-to-toe with a werewolf if I had to. But an undead desert spirit?" I shook my head. "I'm betting the only reason he didn't kill me last night was that he knew a dead reaper would put even worse than me on his trail."

"Probably," Ferryman agreed.

"So are you going to get OtherOps involved now? I've done the work for you. You're practically there." I mentally crossed my fingers.

Ferryman took a long drag at his cigarette, then flicked the butt into the darkness before twirling his fingers to produce another one. "No."

"What do you mean, no?"

"No OtherOps. I want *you* to bring this thing down."

I scoffed. "I just told you: I can't."

"Can't, or won't?"

"What is that supposed to mean?"

Ferryman leaned back in his chair. "Jinn aren't scared of much, but they have a natural aversion toward undead of their own kind."

My mouth went dry. I could feel Maggie recoil. "This has nothing to do with her," I whispered.

"Are you sure?" he asked. "You have a jinn on your finger. I assume that she gives you advice, and I assume that the advice that she gave you is to avoid the ghoul at all costs."

What the fuck is this? Maggie snarled. *A playschool dare? He's trying to goad you into going after a ghoul!*

"Is she wrong?" I challenged Ferryman. He raised his eyebrows at the vehemence of my reply. I cleared my throat, and in a calmer voice, repeated myself. "Is she wrong?"

Ferryman pursed his lips. "Perhaps. Perhaps not. I still have vested interest in catching this creature without the help of a third party." He stared at me expectantly. I got the distinct impression that he wanted *me* to do this, and I couldn't for the life of me figure out why.

"Catching," I said. "*Catching?* I don't think I could even kill it, let alone take it alive."

"I need to know where the rest of the soul mirrors are," Ferryman said. "And I'm willing to pay handsomely."

"You're already paying Ada a fortu…" I trailed off, realizing what he meant.

He gave me his thin-lipped smile and took a drag on his new cigarette. "Finish this job for me, and I will award Ada the agreed-upon price. And I will give you something you want as well. Like the names of your parents."

I took two steps back involuntarily, almost tripping over

my own feet. "You can do that?" I asked quietly.

He nodded.

My contract with Ada is... complicated. She owns me, but that's technically illegal. She bought me from Paronskaft right before they were shut down by OtherOps. The sale was, however, off the books. Even if I were to go to OtherOps and reveal the barcode on my chest and tell them my life story, they wouldn't be able to do a damn thing about it because I don't know the names of my parents. Get the names of my parents, and I might be able to track down the contract. Get the contract, and I could have it annulled by an OtherOps judge.

I could be free.

You can't do it, Maggie said. *If you corner a ghoul in a cemetery, it'll eat you alive.*

What about twilight, when it's regaining its strength?

It's not like a draugr. It'll still be functional, and it'll be pissed that you ruined its sleep.

I stared hard at Ferryman. This didn't even feel real anymore. I'd spent so much time as a slave that the idea of gaining my freedom hadn't even passed through my mind since I was a kid. A thought hit me—the elusive niggle that had been creeping around in the back of my head for days, getting stronger with each moment. I realized it was that information about Kappie owning Judith's offices that set it off.

Maggie, can a ghoul absorb memories?

She seemed taken aback by the question. *I'm not sure. The ability isn't uncommon among shapeshifters, but they'd have to consume the brain. Why do you ask?*

Because that ghoul wasn't trying to kill me back there.

Right, she said. *We established that.*

It pulled me through a house and threw me more than sixty feet. If it wasn't trying to kill me, why did it do that?

To get you away from the imps so he could kill anyone that could identify him.

Maggie, *normal people don't survive that kind of thing. How the hell would it know I'd survive?*

I... *because it knows you're a troll?*

Which is not a secret, but it's not common knowledge, either. There's maybe a dozen people in the state who know what I am. Which means I don't have to fight him in a cemetery at all.

I rounded the table to stand next to Ferryman and unfolded the map. "Okay," I told him. "This is what we're going to do."

A few minutes later, I sat back at my office desk, fingers still pressed against Ferryman's stepping mirror. I grabbed my car keys and wallet and sprinted for the door, passing Nadine with a wave. I peeled out of the parking lot, and as soon as I was on the highway, I called Nadine.

"Forget something, hun?" she asked.

"Nope, just in a hurry."

"What can I do for you?"

"Call the OtherOps morgue. Ask them if an unidentified imp body has passed through there."

"When?"

"Anytime in the last eighteen months. I want to know whether the brain was missing."

"Right on it, hun."

I hung up and eased my seat back a little. I could sense Maggie brooding, no doubt making plans for the eventuality of her ring winding up in the stomach of a ghoul. I looked at the clock. It was ten in the morning. Just a few hours until her anniversary started.

As if she could feel me thinking about her, she spoke up. *You know, you could wait a little while. We can fight it together.*

I was both surprised and touched by the offer. Maggie was always there for me while in her ring, but she'd made it clear since the beginning that her anniversary was *her* time, no matter what. If I couldn't spend it with her, too bad. That she'd offer to spend it gallivanting after a creature that obviously scared her meant a lot.

I can't wait, I said. *If it even suspects that I know who it's been masquerading as, it'll skip town. Shit, it might already be gone.*

I hope it is, she said petulantly.

I don't.

My phone rang. It was Nadine. "Got anything for me?" I asked.

"As a matter of fact, I do. I've got one of their morticians on the other line. He says a mangled imp body came through about eleven months ago. The back of the skull was caved in and the brain was missing. They never ID'd him, and there were no zombie reports in the area, so they did an autopsy and cremated it."

"Does he still have the autopsy report?"

"He's got it in front of him."

"Ask him if the nose was broken. Like, a long time ago."

"Hold on." There was a pause as the line went silent. A minute later, she was back. "That's an affirmative."

"Thanks so much, Nadine." I hung up. "Son of a bitch!" I yelled, slapping the steering wheel.

It's really him? Maggie still seemed skeptical.

"It's definitely him," I breathed aloud. "That shithead, Kappie, has been dead for almost a year. The Kappie Shuteye we spoke to last week was the shapeshifter. He hasn't just been running a secondhand soul business; he took over Kappie's territory completely."

CHAPTER 14

I came to a stop a couple hundred yards from Kappie's crumbling elementary school headquarters and took my time putting on my brand-new flak vest and checking my Glock. I didn't think they'd help all that much, but every little bit counts, doesn't it? Once I'd finished that ritual, I took off through the underbrush around the perimeter of the school parking lot.

This is a terrible plan, Maggie said.

But it is a plan, which is more than I had before. *You sense anything?*

No, she said. *But the ghoul might be actively trying to mask its scent now. It's still sort of a jinn. It has access to powers similar to mine.*

The school was home to Kappie and dozens of imps. The chances of it actually being empty were slim to none, which told me that I'd come to the right place. I reached the rear of the school and watched the windows for a few moments before turning my attention on the loading bay. A semi was parked at the bay—a different truck than last week—but the area looked abandoned despite the door being open.

Here goes nothing. I broke into a sprint, clearing the parking lot and reaching the side of the truck. I checked the cab, then worked my way down the side of the trailer. Weapon at the ready, I rolled into the loading bay and cleared the storage area and then the trailer. There was nothing except a couple of pallets of DVD players, probably stolen.

No one demanded to know what I was doing there. An imp didn't emerge from the school to tell me off. The place was eerily silent.

Do you smell something? Maggie asked.

I sniffed. There was a hint of gasoline. *Semi might be leaking,* I said. Moving quietly, I opened the service door leading away from the storage and was immediately hit by a much stronger, more immediate smell. I took a step inside and found myself in a long, industrial-style kitchen. The place was filthy—pots, pans, and dishes stacked high; old food on the floor; pots of grease discarded beneath stainless steel prep areas. *Never mind*, I said. *The semi is not leaking.*

The reek of gasoline was so powerful that my eyes began to water. My feet splashed, and it took me half a second to realize I was standing in a puddle of the stuff. *This is not good*, I said to Maggie. My first instinct was to get the hell out of there, but I forced myself to keep walking. I rounded the first prep table only to find the gasoline mixing with a pool of blood on the floor. The blood streaked out through the front of the kitchen, as if something had been killed and then dragged elsewhere. There were footprints in the blood.

Big, taloned footprints.

I blinked through the fumes. *You're going to tell me if someone lights a match, right?*

If I say the word hop, *I want you to dive through the closest window*, Maggie replied.

Got it. I followed the trail of blood through the cafeteria and out into one of the main hallways. It continued a few dozen feet, then took an immediate left through a door marked BOILER ROOM. It wasn't the only trail of blood, either. Streaks and drops filled the hallway, all leading to the boiler room. The smell of gas wasn't as bad out here, but I could see that the trail of yellowish liquid lead in the opposite direction. *He's going to burn the place down.*

That's my guess, Maggie agreed.

It's cinder block. What does he expect to accomplish?

He can still gut the place—blow up the kitchen, bring down the roof. It'll be enough to slow down an OtherOps investigation. I eyed the trail of gas but turned to follow the blood instead. I reached the door to the boiler room, the bottoms of my boots slick with crimson. When my hand touched the doorknob, Maggie said, *You don't want to go in there.*

I ignored her and opened the door, stepping through and onto the same catwalk that Kappie had stood on when we'd spoken last week. I had a pretty good idea what to expect, but I made myself look anyway. Beneath the catwalk, at the bottom of the boiler room two stories down, was a pile of very fresh-looking imp corpses. It was the same modus operandi as the meth houses: bodies mutilated beyond recognition, killed quickly and brutally by something much bigger than them. It looked like a scene from the bottom of a butcher's slop bucket.

Somewhere in the distance, I thought I heard a voice. Carefully, I closed the door and returned to the trail of gas, following it down one long hallway, then another. The voice grew louder as I progressed, and I soon realized that someone was singing.

"Taaaaake meeeee ooooooon! Iiiiiii'll beee gooooone!"

I reached the propped-open door to the school gymnasium and stopped just outside, peeking around the corner. The gym was full of pallets of stolen goods, from electronics to toilet paper to power tools. Kappie—or, rather, the ghoul wearing his Kappie suit—stood in the center of the room, gleefully tearing open a pallet of paper towels before dousing the whole thing with fuel from a large gas can.

I could sense Maggie holding her breath.

Anything you want to say before I kick this off? I asked her.

Don't get yourself killed, you big dummy.

Right. See you in a few.

I leaned against the gym door and called out, "Hey, Kappie."

The ghoul spun toward me with a decidedly un-implike growl. Its eyebrows rose, and the side of its face twitched at the sight of me.

"You know," I said, "I would not have expected an undead desert spirit to be a fan of eighties Norwegian synth-pop."

The ghoul discarded the gas can and turned toward me. I

noted that it had an intact left hand. Either the shapeshifter was able to cover up its wounds in a different form, or the limb had regenerated. The second thought did not appeal to me. The creature frowned at me, then seemed to remember what it had been singing. An embarrassed, strangely human smile flickered across its face. "You pick up the strangest things over the course of time." The smile disappeared. "You, Alek Fitz, do not take a hint."

"It's why I'm the best."

"How did you figure out what I was?"

"Because I'm the best."

The ghoul rolled its eyes. "Are you? If you're so smart, why are you still after me?"

"I said I was good, not smart," I answered.

"I let you live last night. I even killed someone you hate." It gestured at the face it was wearing and ran its tongue over its lips. "I saw his memories. I watched him drag little-kid you across a parking lot and shove him into a car. I watched him take the money from your boss. I even felt it when you broke his nose. Kappie was a piece of shit, and you should be thanking me for taking him out of this world."

I fought to suppress long-buried memories and looked toward the ceiling. "You know what? You're right. Thank you."

The ghoul seemed taken aback by my response.

I continued, "I gladly would have crushed his skull myself, if I'd been allowed. I would have drawn the line at eating his brain, though. Imps are nasty."

"You're mocking me?"

"Only a little. I'm genuinely pleased that Kappie is dead. But this thing between you and me has nothing to do with Kappie."

The ghoul took a step back, tensing up, and I realized it was seconds away from shifting into some speedy animal and taking off like it had last night. "There's nothing between you and me," it said.

I gestured at the gym. "Why all this?" I asked.

The sudden question seemed to take the ghoul off guard. It peered at me curiously. "All what?"

"Taking over Kappie's business, stealing souls—*this*."

The shapeshifter seemed to consider the question, and I wondered if anyone had ever inquired after its motives before. "This is the twenty-first century," the ghoul finally said. "There's OtherOps, the Rules, cameras everywhere, high human population density. There aren't many places for someone like me to hide anymore. This was an experiment to see if I could join the rat race, to be something more than just an undead."

The answer surprised me. There was even a tinge of emotion in the ghoul's voice. "That almost sounds romantic when you put it that way—trying to rise above your circumstances."

"That's exactly what it is," the ghoul sniffed. "The Greater Other don't like the undead. They might show some deference to a few of the Vampire Lords, but the rest of us are just gutter trash. They don't want us to get involved in contracts or have a say in the Rules. I'm trying to change that."

"And you thought stealing from Death was a good way to go about it?"

The ghoul shrugged, but I could tell from the shifting of its feet that it *might* have gotten an inkling that this had been a mistake. "I don't know what the big deal is. There's nothing to be afraid of. He's just a dog without a bite."

I thought of something that Maggie had said to me when I'd first met Ferryman in Ada's office. "I've been wondering the same thing myself," I answered. "Why is everyone scared of Death? Seems like a reasonable guy just doing his job. But I've decided it's not about fear. It's about respect."

"There's nothing to respect about him," the ghoul spat. Its

body language no longer spoke of someone ready to run. I had it on the hook now.

"Oh? He's the oldest of the Other—the one being who connects all of us, who has literally seen everything. He takes pains not to interfere with humanity or the rest of the Other, despite his unique position. Seems respectable to me. I don't know. Me? I'm just doing my job, fulfilling another contract. Right now, he's my boss, and he's super fucking pissed at you—so to answer your earlier question, *that* is what's going on between you and me."

"If he's so mad, then why aren't you here with an army?" the ghoul demanded.

"I am the army."

He sputtered a laugh. "You? Really? You're a mixed-blood troll. I've killed full-blood trolls without breaking a sweat."

"Ah!" I replied. "But you haven't killed me. Why? Because you know that OtherOps isn't gonna care all that much about a bunch of dead imps, but they *will* care about a reaper corpse."

The ghoul glared.

I went on, "So here's the deal: no running away. You and me, right now, and let's see how this goes. My investigation? It's all in my head. Shit, I've even got a video of you shifting on my phone. You run away, and I'll hand all of that to OtherOps. You kill me now, and the only trail they have is a bunch of corpses."

You're insane! Maggie said.

The ghoul shifted weight from one foot to the other. Its face shimmered. The creature seemed uncertain.

"Really?" I asked. "You're all big and bad when it comes to slaughtering coked-out imps, but you're a coward when confronted by a man with a gun?"

The ghoul's nostrils flared. The tension in its stance shifted forward, and its body began to shimmer and elongate. Kappie's face and clothing faded, replaced by the mangy hair of the creature I'd tangled with the night before. I didn't wait until the transformation had finished before I emptied my Glock's magazine into the beast's chest.

The ghoul absorbed the bullets with a series of flinches, drawing back two steps before dropping onto all fours and charging me.

I tossed the empty gun aside, squared my shoulders, and extended my tusks. Both my Mjolnir and my Grendel's claw tattoos flared to life. I dropped low, almost overwhelmed by the speed at which the ghoul barreled toward me. I cocked my right arm back, timing for the ghoul's final leap, and swung my right fist with all my strength.

I missed.

The ghoul spun midair, the weight of its body disappearing in exchange for the lithe form of a catlike humanoid. I felt small but razor-sharp talons snag my inner thigh as the beast dropped below my punch and sped past me, jerking me off my feet and throwing me against a pallet of bags of rice. A scream tore itself from my throat, and I looked down to see my torn jeans soaked with an enlarging stain of dark red.

The ghoul scrabbled all four feet on the gym floor, arresting its momentum on a pallet of TVs and turning to leap for me. I saw the shimmer a moment before the change this time, and I rolled out of the way as the heavy brute force of a bull orc slammed into the pallet I'd been leaning against a moment before. The pallet exploded at the impact, rice scattering all across the gym.

The ghoul paused, stunned, and shook its head, letting out the dull moan of a wounded orc. I rolled back toward it, coming up on my knees and slamming Mjolnir into its ribs as hard as I could. It was like punching the bumper of a Buick, but it had the desired effect: the ghoul folded around the impact of the punch and flew six or seven feet into the air, clearing the next pallet and landing on a pile of cereal boxes.

I pressed Maggie's ring against the tear in my thigh.

Cauterize, I ordered.

A flash came out of the ring, and I bit down hard on my tongue as the stench of burning flesh filled my nostrils. I got to my feet, limping as I rounded the destroyed rice pallet and got my sights back on the ghoul.

It transformed again, its body morphing into Kappie, then into the catlike humanoid, then back into the orc, and finally into the mangy creature I'd fought last night. The ghoul rolled onto its stomach and got to its feet, staring me down with the chest-cocked posture of a silverback gorilla. The bullet wounds on its chest were now gone, and it was already moving like the blow I'd given him with Mjolnir was only a minor inconvenience. I clenched my fists and snapped my jaw at him, my tusks growing to their full length. I was seeing red now, and I fought to control the berserker rage that would cloud my judgment.

He's damn slippery, I said to Maggie. *I just need to slow him down for four or five seconds.*

Don't look at me; this is your stupid plan. He's not going to slow down until he's eating your corpse.

The ghoul took one step forward, then paused, sniffing at the air. He slammed one taloned fist on the ground hard enough to shake the floor. "That magic—what is it? Where did it come from?"

Shit, Maggie said. *He smells me.*

I rushed forward, fists swinging. The ghoul pounded the ground twice and rushed to meet me. He deftly avoided a blow from my right fist, but that was only a feint to take his attention off my left. My Grendel's claw tattoo flared, sorcery slicing through his meaty stomach and coming up to take his arm off at the shoulder. The ghoul screamed, snatching me with his good arm faster than I could follow and lifting me clear off the ground before slamming me against the floor like a toy.

A rainbow of pain exploded behind my eyes as I tried

desperately to suck in the oxygen that had just been dashed from my lungs. The ghoul's face grew large in my addled vision, its jaws snapping. I tried to swing my left hand again, but I found my arms pinned by a new pair of pink, hairless arms that had sprouted from the ghoul's torso.

I head-butted him, my tusks connecting with his teeth. He roared but did not let go. Great wads of bloody drool dripped from his mouth onto my face. "Where is that magic coming from?" the ghoul demanded. "Where is the jinn?" The creature lifted me by my flak vest and slammed me into the ground to punctuate each word. "I will not let you die until you tell me where to find him!"

I could barely think, let alone move. My struggles grew weaker. I just couldn't deal with the strength of such an ancient spirit. I tried to reach for my pocket, unsuccessfully. *Maggie*, I managed mentally, *I think you were right. This was a bad idea.*

She didn't answer.

A sudden noise arrested the flurry of violence. It took me a moment to recognize it: a da-nah-nah-nah repeating over and over again. It was my phone alarm. During the fight, my phone must have fallen from my pocket, and now it was going off from somewhere by the ruined pallet of rice.

I choked out a laugh and saw specks of blood appear on the tips of my tusks.

"What is that?" the ghoul demanded.

"That," I said, "means you're out of time."

"What?"

Over the ghoul's shoulder, I saw a trickle of crimson and orange smoke. It shimmered and coalesced into an olive-skinned woman who looked to be in her midtwenties. She was around five foot six, with long black hair tied neatly over one shoulder. She was stark naked, and she looked *super* annoyed.

The ghoul dropped me and spun toward her, a new arm

growing from the stump of his left as quickly as he could swing it. Maggie batted it away with a petite hand, her feet barely shifting, and reached out to grab the ghoul by his bottom jaw. The undead's body flailed in her grip, its mangy fur shimmering as it struggled to change.

"Alek, now!" Maggie called.

I summoned everything I could manage and pulled Ferryman's stepping mirror out of my pocket. I slapped it against the ground, then grabbed a handful of the ghoul's fur and pressed three fingers against the mirror. The effect was instantaneous. The world went black, every noise suddenly gone, as if we had been swallowed by a cave deep inside the earth. I could still feel the ghoul's fur in my hand. There was a hesitant snuffling noise, and suddenly I was snatched up again.

"What is this?" the ghoul roared. "Where am I?"

"Put him down, little dog," a voice said calmly.

I was cast aside, and suddenly a light flickered into being. It was the one on Ferryman's damn card table. He sat behind it, dealing out a new game of solitaire. The light of the lamp barely touched the ghoul's face, casting its body in dangerous shadows. "Who are you?" the ghoul demanded.

Ferryman looked up, but he wasn't an old man in the AC/DC T-shirt anymore—he was a grinning skull. "I'm the one thing you never wanted to meet."

The ghoul hesitated. For the first time, I saw real fear in its eyes. It took one step back into the darkness, then another, snuffling cautiously. "Get me out of here," it said to me. "Get me out!"

"You may go," the skull told me.

I blinked, and I was back in the gymnasium, lying on the floor in a slick puddle of blood and rice. I craned by head to search for Maggie, only to find her procuring a large hoodie from one of the pallets of stolen goods. She pulled it over her head, turned, and spotted me. Running over, she exclaimed,

"Holy shit, Alek, are you okay?"

Everything hurt. It was worse than the car accident by far. Even the muscles in my fingers and toes felt like they'd been crushed beneath a boulder. I flexed my arms to make sure they'd still move and checked my thigh. Even with Maggie's cauterization, it still bled. I took a deep breath, receiving a sharp pain in my chest as a reward.

"Cracked ribs," I told her. "Probably cracked other things. I should probably get some X-rays." I forced my tusks back down and let her help me off the ground. I blinked against the pain and took a close look at her. Her eyes were bloodshot, her face haggard. "Are *you* okay?"

"I shouldn't expend that kind of energy right out of the ring," she said with a weak smile. "I'll be okay, but I'm glad you could still move, because I wouldn't have been able to hold him for more than a few seconds."

I pulled her into a hug. "That's all that I needed," I said.

"Delivery made?" she asked.

"Delivery made," I confirmed.

She put her shoulder beneath my arm, waving away my protests even though I could tell she was swaying on her feet. "Let's get you to a hospital."

"I'll be okay," I told her. "Help me to the car. We have somewhere to be."

Chapter 15

We arrived at a nameless little beach on the coast of South Carolina at about six o'clock in the morning. The very first rays of the sun were visible over the rolling ocean, and as I pulled into the parking lot, I stopped to look at Maggie's small form curled up in the passenger seat. Her face was serene, the wrinkles gone. A little real-world sleep had returned her strength in a way that I could only be jealous of. My own body was a mess. Breathing hurt. Talking hurt. Driving hurt. I'd almost passed out three times on the drive down, but I'd be damned if I ever told Maggie that.

I gently touched her shoulder and watched her eyes flicker open.

She sat up slowly. "Where are we?" she asked, and froze in midstretch as she spotted the beach. She let out the kind of squeal one might expect from a little girl opening Christmas presents rather than from a seven-hundred-year-old jinn. She threw the car door open, stripped off her pilfered hoodie, and ran naked toward the beach, diving into an oncoming wave without hesitation.

I couldn't help but grin as I slowly pulled myself out of the car and walked gingerly out onto the sand. Someone had left behind a folding beach chair. I sank into it and put my head back, watching Maggie as she frolicked in the surf like a kid. I lay there peacefully as the sun rose, until I felt the heat of my barcode suddenly cut through all my other pains.

I pulled out my phone. It was crusted with dried blood that I had to wipe away to see that I had nine messages from the past twenty-four hours. One was from Justin, two from Nadine, and six were from Ada. A shiver of fear went through my belly that I'd somehow screwed up—that the job wasn't finished and she was going to kill me for running out in the middle of work. My mouth dry, I dialed her number.

"Where the hell are you?" she asked.

"I'm in South Carolina," I told her.

"*Excuse me?*"

"I had a promise to keep to a friend."

I could feel her glaring through the phone. "Ferryman called last night," she said without pressing further.

"And?"

"He paid in full. He said you did an amazing job and that I should treat you better."

I swallowed the lump in my throat. "I don't disagree," I replied.

"Whatever. Don't be a prick about it. He said you're hurt?"

"Yeah. Some cuts. Probably a bunch of cracked bones. A lot of blunt-force trauma."

"What did you fight that can crack *your* bones?"

"A ghoul."

"I don't know what the hell that is." She gave a long-suffering sigh. "Fine. You have the next five days off. I expect you back in the office by Thursday. And you can…" she muttered something under her breath.

"I can what?" I asked. Five days? That was unheard of. Ferryman must have paid her an absolute fortune.

"You can have bank holidays off this year. Ferryman's request. Seems he knows about our little arrangement and thought I should throw you a bone. This year only, mind! Enjoy your damn trip." She hung up.

I checked Nadine's messages, but she was just trying to let me know that Ada was looking for me. Finally, I listened to the message from Justin. It was from Thursday morning.

"Hey, bud," it said. "Mission accomplished. You necromancer buddy demanded his phone call about half hour after you left. He talked to a woman named Kimberly Donavon. From the sound of things, she's definitely the one who hired him. Normally, we'd go after her ourselves right away, but I figured you might want first stab, so I put it off until Wednesday. Nick is back in solitary, so she has no idea you're coming. I texted you her address."

I called him back and thanked him, making sure that I still had the rest of the weekend before OtherOps made their move. I did.

Maggie returned, dripping, a half hour later. I was half asleep when she dropped none-so-gently into my lap.

"Ow!" I said.

"Oh! Sorry about that." She grinned at me. "I haven't been swimming for five centuries, Alek. Five centuries!" She leapt back to her feet, throwing her hands in the air. The wind whipped off the Atlantic, but she barely seemed to notice the spring cold.

"Sorry we've blown through most of your anniversary," I said, glancing at the clock on my phone. "What do you want to do for the rest of it?"

"You sure you don't need a hospital?" she said, sobering.

"I think I can get through another six or seven hours."

"Good. Let's get shit-faced and spend the rest of the morning in a hammock."

"That," I said, "is the best idea I've ever heard."

Epilogue

The three-story, white stucco house sat on a quiet, old-moneyed street in Cleveland Heights, just a stone's throw from my favorite Thai place in Coventry. It was the type of hundred-year-old house I used to dream of owning someday, back when I went on ride-alongs with the old reapers as a kid. I stood in the street outside, leaning against my rental while Maggie took stock of the place.

I don't sense anything out of the ordinary, she said. *No wards, no sorcery, no bodyguards. There's one lady in there, probably in her midfifties. She's watching soap operas.*

It was four o'clock on Monday afternoon. I'd managed to get back from South Carolina without passing out, and I'd spent most of Sunday in the hospital. The ghoul had cracked pretty much everything in my body, but Ada's personal doctor had given me a bunch of heavy painkillers and told me that my troll blood would heal it all within a month or two, which didn't seem all that useful to me.

We're good, Maggie concluded. *Either she's so goddamned powerful that not even I can sense her sorcery, or she's just an ordinary person.*

Why would an ordinary person hire a necromancer to kill me?

Because they can't do it themselves? Technically, she hired the necromancer to bring her my *ring.* There was menace in Maggie's voice.

Let me take care of this, I told her.

She snorted.

I walked up the short drive and knocked on the door, listening to the soap opera playing through the living room window. I was wearing a Valkyrie Collections hoodie over my flak jacket, the hood pushed back, one hand ready to reach for my gun. I saw a curtain shift, then heard footsteps inside.

The door opened to reveal a blonde-haired woman with crow's-feet in the corners of her eyes and a heavily made-up face. She looked more tired than menacing, and she gave me a single glance before letting out a sigh. "It's you," she said.

"Hi." I managed a smile, even though I didn't feel like it. "Kimberly Donavon?"

She glanced past me, into the street. Her jaw tightened, and she lifted her chin toward me. "You going to kill me?" she asked.

I tongued at the torn-up gums of my bottom canines. "Can we talk inside?"

"Might as well," she said with a shrug, turning and walking away.

I followed her inside, shutting the door behind me and heading into the living room, where she turned off her soaps and dropped into the couch. Despite the exhaustion in her face, there was an edge of defiance. "Well?" she asked. "Get on with it."

I looked around the living room. Everything about it screamed upper-middle-class family home, from the baby grand piano centerpiece to the big-screen TV over the fireplace to the expensive-looking suede couches. There was no hint of anything out of the ordinary. No sign of the Other. "Get on with what?"

"Whatever you people do to people like me."

I took a deep breath. "What do you think I am?"

"I have no idea. All I know is that fool kid Nick couldn't bring me what I paid for and landed himself in an OtherOps lockup." She scowled. "How did you find me? They trace the call? I figured they'd do that the moment I hung up the phone. Been waiting all weekend for someone to show up. So what'll it be? Torture? Maiming? Death? I assume you're friends with some pretty powerful people to keep Nick locked up." She spoke a thousand words a minute, one sentence bleeding into the next, barely stopping to take a breath.

Jesus, Maggie said. *She is an absolute mess.* There was actually a note of sympathy in her tone.

I noticed Kimberly's eyes flick down to Maggie's ring. I turned the armchair away from the TV and sat down across from her, lacing my fingers. "I'm not going to kill you," I said gently.

"Why not? I tried to kill you."

"You tried to steal from me," I corrected her. "The fact that your errand boy decided to make things violent wasn't your fault."

"It was," she insisted. "I told him to get me the jinn at all costs. I wouldn't have batted an eye if he'd killed you."

"You're not very good at poker, are you?"

"What?"

"Never mind." I drummed one fingernail against a lower canine. "Why do you want the jinn?"

A flurry of emotions crawled across Kimberly's face: guilt, anger, relief, hatred, revulsion. She had a million different things bottled up in that head of hers. I couldn't imagine what had caused them. Her eyes moved to Maggie's ring again. "Is that it?" she asked. "Her vessel?"

Oh, no, Maggie suddenly said.

My attention split between the two. I covered the ring with one hand and said to Maggie, *What's wrong?*

I just figured out who this is. Look at the picture on the piano over there.

Instead of answering Kimberly's question, I got up and casually paced the room, letting my eyes play across the photo Maggie had pointed out. The quality wasn't great—probably taken fifteen or twenty years ago. It showed a well-dressed man in his midthirties leaning against a tree, laughing. *Who is that?* I asked Maggie.

She fell silent. Across from me, Kimberly shifted on the couch, her face twisting into a grimace. "I wanted the ring for revenge," she said.

It was my turn to be caught off guard. I turned away from the piano. "Revenge for what?"

She sniffed and got up from the couch, crossing to the photo. She stood beside me, plucking it from the piano and practically shoving it into my hands. "For him. For my baby brother." I looked at the photo, wondering if I was supposed to be getting all of this. Maggie wouldn't speak up, which meant I was the only person in the room completely in the dark.

"She killed him," Kimberly said.

"Who?"

"That *creature* in your ring. She turned him inside out and left his corpse to rot in the gutter."

"Wha..." I didn't know what to say. Maggie couldn't *do* that. I was pretty sure I knew the limitations of her powers from within the ring. She could set people on fire with her sorcery at close range, but turning them inside out wasn't on her list of tricks. "How the hell do you know any of this?" I asked. "Who *are* you?"

"Just a woman who wants her brother back." She snatched the picture away from me and returned it lovingly to her piano, then paced the floor. "I *didn't* know any of this. Not until a few months ago. I've spent the last decade thinking my little brother had been murdered by hoodlums or thieves. But a man came to me—an old man. He claimed he was some kind of magician. He *showed* me the truth that the jinn killed my brother. He said that he was the one who'd put her in that ring, and if I got the ring for him, he would allow me my vengeance."

Maggie, what is going on?

She remained quiet.

"Why would you trust this guy?" I asked Kimberly. "Some stranger you never met, claiming to know magic..."

Kimberly shifted anxiously. She leaned toward me, as if it were of vital importance that I know she was being truthful.

"I just *knew*. He showed me things. It was like watching a movie in my own brain, like living the events myself." She blinked rapidly, tears forming in the corners of her eyes. "He showed me what that bitch did to my brother."

I was getting fed up with Maggie's silence. There wasn't a lie in Kimberly's anxious eyes, but I had a hard time believing Maggie was capable of what she claimed. "This magician," I asked, "did he leave some way to contact him?"

Kimberly swallowed hard, then fetched her purse from the other end of the couch. She fished around inside for a few moments before handing me a white card. It had a phone number on it and the name MATTHIAS in small letters in top right-hand corner. "That's him. He said not to bother going to OtherOps—that the jinn had power over the cops." Kimberly paused, staring at Maggie's ring. Her fingers twitched toward it, ever so slightly, and then her entire body sagged in defeat. "This isn't my world," she said, finally averting her eyes to stare into the middle distance. "I shouldn't have gotten involved. I should have known better."

"Yes, you should have."

"What are you going to do to me?"

"To you? Nothing. You're just a patsy. I recommend that when OtherOps comes by you deny everything. All they have is a single phone call." The last thing I needed was OtherOps sniffing around Maggie's ring. I held up the business card between two fingers. "I'm going to find your magician friend and smash his face in. You're done with this business. You get involved again, and there won't be any second chances. Understand?"

"I understand."

"Good." I felt a swirl of anger and pity. Someone had gotten to this lady—someone who could convince her that Maggie was a killer. Maybe it was one of my enemies, maybe it was one of Maggie's, but a magician had tried to use this lady to grab the ring. It made my blood boil. I left before

I could get any angrier and got in the car. I leaned the seat back, trying to cool down.

Maggie, do you have any idea what's going on?

There was a long, terrible silence. I willed her to deny everything. To respond. To make any sort of noise.

It's true, she finally said.

What's true? I asked.

Her brother. I killed him, just like she claims. Maggie's voice was flat, devoid of emotion.

What the hell? I was blindsided. I couldn't think through my own confusion. This wasn't her. It couldn't be. She might not talk much about her past, but I felt like I'd gotten to know what type of person she was over the last ten years, and I couldn't even imagine her doing such a thing.

He had the ring before you. He was an amateur magician, and he had an artifact he could use to amplify my power and control it. He thought I was his little genie in a bottle. He thought I was a slave to be used and abused. A snarl entered her tone. *One year, during my anniversary, I got him drunk and killed him. I took the ring and hid it. And then you found it.*

I was speechless. I *definitely* didn't know that she could kill the person who was wearing her ring.

Maggie continued, her voice level again. *That woman in there has no idea that her brother was a practitioner or a sleaze. To her, he was just her baby brother; an innocent murdered by an ancient evil.* I could sense the belief in her words, feel her grief. She let out a long, trembling sigh. *God damn it. How is he still alive? Why did he bring her into it?*

Wait, who is still alive? I thought you killed him.

Not my last ring bearer, Matthias—the asshole magician who put me in here. He's still alive, and now he's trying to get my ring back. Damn it! I'm not going to let him hurt you or take my ring. Alek, you've got to get me out of here.

I sat in a deli on the east side, a half-eaten Reuben in front of me, my appetite gone after my confrontation with Kimberly. Maggie hadn't spoken since, and I didn't know what to say to her. I always knew she was powerful, of course, but the idea that she could kill the person who carried her ring terrified me. I became aware of a complacency that I didn't even know was there; I felt like a fool for being fast, loose, and friendly with an ancient creature from the Other.

It also meant that I was now part of whatever game this Matthias was playing. To come after her, he would have to go through me. Maggie was still my best friend. I wouldn't have it any other way. But I *would* have liked the opportunity to make that choice for myself.

I looked up as the diner doorbell rang, and Ferryman strolled inside. He walked over, paused dramatically, and looked at me over a pair of sunglasses. He took a long drag from his cigarette and crushed it out under his boot, then dropped into the seat across the table.

"You have a pep in your step today," I said.

He grinned. "Everything is how it should be—the souls are recovered; no more shades are dying; my realm has stabilized; your boss is paid; and the Lords of Hell are happy to have their property back."

I took a bite of my Reuben even though I didn't want to. After I swallowed, I said, "I appreciate you telling Ada to give me bank holidays off. It might sound dumb, but… I really do appreciate it."

"It was nothing. Consider it a tip."

I hesitated. "I thought we had arranged something else as a tip."

"Indeed we had. I am a man of my word, after all." Ferryman rotated his fingers, and one of his business cards appeared between them. He rotated the fingers of the other hand to produce a pen. He clicked it once and scribbled something on the card before pushing it over to me.

I looked down. "Magnus and Anita Johnson," I read aloud. Saying the names seemed to bring a hush over my body, every muscle frozen as if they were holy—or unholy—things. "Do you have anything else?" I asked.

Ferryman tapped the side of his nose. "The agreed price was two names."

"Johnson is the most common name in the country," I said.

"Second-most common name," Ferryman corrected.

"Are they dead?"

Ferryman considered the question for a moment. "I appreciate everything you did—the risk you took—but you must understand that I, above all Others, am restricted in how I can interact with your world. I've given you two names. One of them has passed through my realm. I can say no more."

"Well," I said, looking down at the names. Which of them was still alive, and which had passed on? I'd have to figure that out on my own. It wasn't much, but it was something. "Thanks?"

"You're welcome." Ferryman paused. "You have another question."

I tapped the card thoughtfully and looked up to meet his eyes. "I know I shouldn't look a gift horse in the mouth and all that... but why would you ask Ada to give me extra time off?" Ferryman cocked an eyebrow. I could have sworn his eyes twinkled. It might have just been the rotation of the galaxies contained within them. "Why the kindness?" I clarified.

"Because it cost me nothing but some noise muttered into a phone," Ferryman said. "If you care to be romantic, I did it because kindness is not solely a human trait." He leaned forward slightly. "If you care to be cynical, it's because we may work together again some day. A good business relationship is the best kind of business relationship." He grinned.

I laughed and glanced down at the card once more. When I looked up, Ferryman was gone, leaving behind the faint odor of cigarette smoke.

I sat for some time, thinking about the names on the card. I wondered why they'd sold me all those years ago; whose idea it had been; what they'd gotten in return. I wondered which of them was dead, and if I'd ever find them. I didn't know if I wanted to actually confront them. I was, after all, looking for a contract rather than a person.

Maggie.

I felt her presence move around in the ring.

I continued without waiting for an answer. *I don't know about your past. I don't really care. But you're my friend. I'll do everything I can to get you out of that ring.*

I know, she said quietly. *I'm sorry I didn't tell you earlier.*

It's none of my business, I assured her.

I know it's not really my fault—you put on the ring, after all—but with Matthias still alive, I've now dragged you into something bigger. Get me out of here, and I'll use all my powers to break the contract that binds you to Ada. This I swear.

I smiled. I didn't have much, but I did have friends. *It's a deal.*

For more from Brian McClellan:

Promise of Blood
The Powder Mage Trilogy
Orbit, April 2013

The Crimson Campaign
The Powder Mage Trilogy
Orbit, May 2014

The Autumn Republic
The Powder Mage Trilogy
Orbit, February 2015

Sins of Empire
Gods of Blood and Powder
Orbit, March 2017

Wrath of Empire
Gods of Blood and Powder
Orbit, May 2018

Blood of Empire
Gods of Blood and Powder
Orbit, November 2019

Contact Brian McClellan

Website: brianmcclellan.com
Twitter: twitter.com/BrianTMcClellan
Facebook: facebook.com/briantmcclellan
Goodreads: goodreads.com/brianmcclellan
brian@brianmcclellan.com

Acknowledgements

Shen Fey - cover artist
Shawn King - cover design
Daniel Friend - line editor
Kristy Stewart - copy editor

Special Thanks to Michele McClellan, David Wohlreich, Adam N, William Neil Scott, Jarett Furr, Nicole Sanborn, Michelle Potter, Laurie Bell, Barbara Soares, Mark Lindberg, Kelly Bowers, Wyatt Nevins, Nicole Evans, Elizabeth Jarvis, Tiffany Renee, Sam Baskin, Thomas Flott, Brenden, Leticia Lara, Mitchell Coomber, Rebecca Razza, Aprilynne Pike, Scott Hurff, Lee West, Benjamin Dunn, Ravi Persaud, Josh Arcelo, Lois Young, Daniel Chesmore, Joseph Hall, Zarin Ficklin, JS Lenore, Chris Chabot, Kristina Pick, MM Schill, Kirstie Paul, Linda Yuan, Chanie Beckman, Adrianne Cavaioli, Adaya Viera